7/23

Praise for *The Apartment*

"A dazzling inquiry into the disquietudes of time and place, of past and present, and the global exiles who inhabit the realms in between. Menéndez's exquisitely wrought stories—emanating from the life span of one modest Miami apartment—offer us no less than the world. A masterful, poetic achievement."

—Cristina García, author of *Dreaming in Cuban*

"Stunning in its intimate yet vast portrayal of humanity, *The Apartment* tenderly summons the power of our bonds to place and community, evoking the grace of human connections that save us time and time again. A balm for our deeply divided times."

—Richard Blanco, presidential inaugural poet, author of *The Prince of Los Cocuyos: A Miami Childhood*

"Ana Menéndez gives us an intimate, picturesque tale that grows into a mysterious and supernatural journey through time as the conflicted narrators become ghosts and echoes of each other. Striking and haunting, this powerful novel battles between gut-wrenchingly lonely and harrowing moments in America and the multifaceted, resilient, and radically caring community that has blossomed against them. It's a reminder that we breathe new air everyday, that we are always connected to each other, that we survive when we stick together."

—Xochitl Gonzalez, author of *Olga Dies Dreaming*

"Menéndez writes from the gut, expertly crafting the tensions and bitterness of misplacement, the suffocation of place. She also writes from the spleen; Menéndez's acerbic wit finds its way interstitially through the pages of this book, finding another gear for an already beautiful prose. The array of characters, all of whom have jumped out of a frying pan and into a fire, and specifically, into apartment 2B of the Helena, are escaping a past that won't let them be. They're immigrants and refugees whose hopelessness at times obfuscates their political realities: here isn't always better than there. At the center of this book, Menéndez has constructed a home, a building, a city; she's also drawn a line—possibly a circle—that stretches from imperialism to mental health."

—Alejandro Varela, author of *The People Who Report More Stress*

"Ingenious in its construction, intimate in its storytelling, and illuminating in its insights, *The Apartment* is both an unforgettable reading experience and a fascinating character in itself: like the mysterious stranger next door whose history, hopes, longings, secrets, and surprises thrillingly reveal themselves over time."

—Christopher Castellani, author of *Leading Men*

"Ana Menéndez should be donned the poet laureate of South Beach—not the South Beach of Versace mansions and trendy nightclubs but a more human place where wanderers seek the kind of quotidian security that often proves so elusive for us all. *The Apartment* is a jewel of a novel that dares question the very notion of what we consider home—a stunning meditation on the ghosts we leave behind and the phantoms that are perennially our companions in exile"

—Ernesto Mestre-Reed, author of *Sacrificio*

"An exquisite palimpsest of culture, memory, and place, Ana Menéndez's *The Apartment* is the *Canterbury Tales* of Miami Beach. A series of vivid, original characters move in and out of apartment 2B, each of them inscribing it with their indelible stories. Rendered in elegant, masterful prose, this novel will enthrall readers and haunt them long after the last page."

—Diana Abu-Jaber, author of *Fencing with the King*

The
Apartment

ALSO BY ANA MENÉNDEZ

Adios, Happy Homeland!

The Last War

Loving Che

In Cuba I Was a German Shepherd

The Apartment

A NOVEL

Ana Menéndez

COUNTERPOINT

BERKELEY

First Counterpoint edition: 2023

Library of Congress Cataloging-in-Publication Data
Names: Menéndez, Ana, 1970- author.
Title: The apartment : a novel / Ana Menéndez.
Description: First Counterpoint edition. | Berkeley : Counterpoint, 2023.
Identifiers: LCCN 2022058973 | ISBN 9781640095830 (hardcover) | ISBN 9781640095847 (ebook)
Subjects: LCGFT: Novels.
Classification: LCC PS3563.E514 A66 2023 | DDC 813/.54—dc23/eng/20221209
LC record available at https://lccn.loc.gov/2022058973

Jacket design by Jaya Miceli
Jacket photographs of apartment © Littleny / Alamy Stock Photo,
woman © Shutterstock / hxdbzxy
Book design by Laura Berry

COUNTERPOINT
2560 Ninth Street, Suite 318
Berkeley, CA 94710
www.counterpointpress.com

Printed in the United States of America

1 3 5 7 9 10 8 6 4 2

In memory of my grandmothers

There is no face that is not on the verge of blurring and fading away like the faces in a dream. Everything in the world of mortals has the value of the irrecoverable and contingent.

—Jorge Luis Borges

The dead, after all, do not walk backwards but they do walk behind us. They have no lungs and cannot call out but would love for us to turn around. They are victims of love, many of them.

—Anne Carson

A serpent coils through the underbrush of palmetto and coco plum. It's a still, dry afternoon, so the woman hears the creature before she sees it. A crackle of brown leaves, like a fire starting. She stops, instinctively raises her basket of turtle eggs. Death wouldn't be so bad as the loss of the evening meal. She scans the mesh of roots. A flash of red and yellow, and the woman goes cold. But then the small bands of black slide into view as the snake undulates past. The woman relaxes her arms. Harmless, this one. This time.

She doesn't count the years the way the strangers who have begun appearing on these shores count the years. Next season, a new traveler will appear, body covered with too much clothing, like all his kind. He will introduce himself as Menéndez de Avilés. The following season, the woman's mother will struggle to breathe for five nights and then die. Others will develop the same strange sickness. Generations later, the weakened tribe will fall to the invading Uchises and Yamases. The survivors will flee to a great new city called Havana, where most of them will die. The survivors of the survivors will return, thin and scarred. More clothed men will arrive to build first one hut, then another along the sea-facing shore. Then great machines, of the kind the woman cannot imagine, will occupy this slender island. Men will lay down planks to ride their machines from the mainland.

By then the woman's tribe will have vanished from this

barrier island. Their three souls—eyes, shadows, reflections—will be left to wander without rest. The only evidence that they lived will be a mound of skulls that a future tribe of speculators will uncover a half day's walk north of the spot where, on this day of the distant past, the woman gathers her family's meal. To her, time is ripples on the water's surface, concentric circles that form and re-form: The season of biting insects, the season of storms, the season of turtle eggs, the season of blue skies, and then the season of biting insects, the storms, the turtle eggs . . . The world turning again and again, just as every day the sun rises from the water and sets in the land. She can't know that the crocodiles and the rabbits will vanish. Snails and lobsters will no longer crowd the bay. Wildcats and bears won't hunt in the thickets. Deer will disappear, along with the pigeon plums and the palm nuts, the gopher apples. Water holes will dry up. Men will pull out the mangrove roots. The palmetto and sabal will be replaced by coconut and avocado—making this a land of permanent occupation.

Here, where the woman disturbs the burrowing creatures, in this same patch where she pauses to listen to the sea's roar, many years from now workers will cut a path by hand. A street will cover the wound. A man named William will buy a plot. And an architect named Henry will design a two-story building. He'll name it the Helena, after his mother, who told him stories to help him sleep.

Neither William nor Henry nor the day laborers who slashed their forearms on palmetto blades, nor the generations who will come to live in the Helena, can ever know about the woman collecting the eggs of nesting sea turtles this evening. And she, who turns herself now to the wind, under a strangely yellowing sky, cannot know about them.

But you who exist outside of time, look: The setting sun drops its boulder of night. Within heartbeats, the land disappears. In the morning, out of the mangroves rise hundreds of new buildings, smooth and whiter than sand—dazzling in their monstrous beauty.

SOPHIE, 1942

The building, begun in 1940, is not quite finished by the time Sophie moves into apartment 2B on January 8, 1942. THE HELENA, announce the block letters over the entrance. And Sophie, who has just abandoned a classics degree, is amused. Fitting that the woman whose face launched a thousand ships to war should ghost over this, the first Miami Beach apartment building requisitioned by the military. For the next several months, maybe years (no one really knows how long this war will last), the Helena will be home to fifteen lieutenant colonels, majors, and captains of the U.S. Army Air Corps. At least one of them, Major Jack Appleton, directly assisting Lt. Col. James Stowell, will arrive with a new bride.

Apartment 2B is on the second floor, with windows on the north and south. It has a simple layout, typical of its time: The front door opens into the living room. Ahead, a narrow hallway leads to the bedrooms, a small one toward the back, and over the street a larger one that features a large built-in closet, an innovation that eliminates the need for armoires. Off the living room, to the south, is a small dining room and behind that a galley kitchen with a door that leads to the back stairs. When Sophie moves in, apartment 2B still smells of fresh paint and all the interior doors are missing. Eventually she will grow tired of waiting for the army to hang doors and she'll hang the door to the master bedroom herself. But at least there's some furniture: a daveno in the main bedroom, and in the living room a reclining chair that Jack shipped ahead from San Antonio. The kitchen cabinets hold two pots and a cast-iron saucepan. The dishware is the kind you buy with green stamps, so Sophie's glad that, against Jack's wishes, she's brought her grandmother's china, decorated with small blue flowers, and the set of Glo-tone tableware from Sears, Roebuck they received as a wedding gift. The place is comfortable enough. And whatever the apartment's deficiencies, the view beyond its casement windows always delights. Miami Beach!

This is the eerie thing: Last June in San Antonio, she and Jack had gone to the pictures to see Betty Grable and Don Ameche in *Moon over Miami*. Sophie was enchanted. And for days she sang "Oh me, oh my! Miami!" Until Jack told her to shut up already. But that old fuddy-duddy couldn't stop her from dreaming herself at the Palm Grove, dancing in a gold lamé halter, singing, "Susana is still in Havana . . ." Poor Betty, stuck in Texas just like Sophie. Oh, to be in Miami. A silly dream. And then, like that, it happened! The Japanese attacked Pearl Harbor, and a week later Jack received his orders to lead the officers' school down in Miami Beach. When Jack told her the news, Sophie fainted straightaway. She didn't dare believe in a power that could summon fate.

Over those first days, before the recruits arrive, she and Jack lose themselves between the sheets at night, the windows opened to the balmy breeze. Soon, though, Jack is spending all his mornings out at the golf course, where every day new boys arrive for their training. Some nights he doesn't even return to the Helena. So Sophie spends the evenings on her own, strolling down to the beach, sometimes taking in a movie. Saturday nights, when Jack is home, they'll walk down to the new Clevelander Hotel for a gin and tonic. There is still space in this war for leisure—distance dilutes violence the way water tames alcohol. All of them waiting in a state of edgy inebriation.

In the beginning, they are happy. The world roils, but the Helena's happy shell seems to enclose a remarkably egalitarian village. Here every apartment is identical to every other one, laid out back-to-back in mirror images on either side of the supporting beams. Each two-bedroom, one-bath leaning on its neighbor—dining room to dining room, kitchen to kitchen. Up and down the stairs of the Helena: Everyone a transplant from somewhere else; everyone united in the war effort.

SOME DAYS, WHEN THERE'S A STRONG NORTH wind, the smell of gunpowder fills the apartment. And the distant low boom of practice artillery on the beach quickens

Sophie's heart. She is the new wife of a handsome major, and his war has become hers as surely as her life has become his. Sophie is now inseparable from her husband. She has neither credit nor domicile in her own name, which, anyway, is no longer hers. When the army transferred Jack to Miami Beach, Sophie did not hesitate to leave her studies, marry, and accompany her husband on the two-day drive south. New adventures! The promise of a new apartment to decorate, a new landscape, a brand-new self, fitted first to her husband and then to the wider calling of the war. A heroic life, such as any she could imagine for herself.

Miami Beach resplendently green. Amid so much preparation for war, so much life, such joy! The gaiety intoxicates her more than the Ronrico daiquiris at Mother Kelly's. Plans and men are afoot. The air itself reflects the light. And one night, by the Beachcomber, they even see Clark Gable! Well, Sophie is certain it's Clark Gable. Jack says she's acting like a silly girl from Plano, which is what she is. And why was she looking around at the faces of the men anyway? It's true that Jack has his temper, but who wouldn't in his circumstances? When he returns from the war, things will be well. They'll start a family. Sophie will be more careful when she speaks. For now, there are the evening strolls up Alton Road with Jack, who is so handsome, more handsome even than Clark Gable, with a way of being that bewitches everyone.

That first month in Miami Beach unspools like a movie, a Technicolor spectacle where distant fighting means suffering only in the abstract. And Sophie thinks she understands why men go to war, generation after generation: war is a thrilling break in the routine of every day.

In February, a German U-boat strikes the *Pan Massachusetts* off Cape Canaveral and blackouts hit the beach. When Sophie forgets to close the venetians, Jack throws a glass at her. She kneels at his feet and weeps. Sometimes she has butterflies for brains. She's so very, very sorry. That night, for the first time that Sophie can recall, Jack begins to grind his teeth in his sleep. Sophie nudges him, and he's on her, quick as a breath.

"Stop, stop! You're suffocating me," she yells. Jack wakes, startled, but immediately covers her mouth with his hand.

"Shut up, you little fool. You want to wake the whole building?"

In the morning, he is his loving self again. *My crumpet, my sweet. Your dear Jackie adores you.* But the redness around Sophie's mouth doesn't fade until lunchtime.

A week later, she dreams he does it again. She feels his body cover hers, but she cannot move. She cannot even scream—paralysis overcomes her, and Sophie is certain she will die. Darkness as the pillow covers her face. Her throat closes against sound and breath until at the last moment she wakes, gasping. Jack asleep quietly beside her.

One morning in May, Sophie wakes before dawn. Some sound below, something moving in the street. The blinds are tight against the open window, but the breeze carries the promise of fire. The voices of men drift in with the smoke. She looks back to the room where Jack sleeps, and then to the blinds. She takes a deep breath and raises one of the slats.

"What the hell are you doing?" Jack's voice.

Sophie stands, squares her body.

"Something's burning."

"Get back to bed."

"No."

She follows him down the stairs and past the guards stationed in front.

"Neutral tanker," one of the boys tells them. "German torpedoes hit it overnight."

They run with the others. A crowd rims the shore. Sophie brings her hands to her mouth. The tanker drifts north, a giant torch in the water. Sophie loses Jack in the crowd.

"Crude oil," says an old man standing next to her. "The war's come home, sister."

Day breaks. A pale sky frames the black smoke. It billows and grows over the wounded ship, roiling like an inverted dark sea. The stench has made some people cover their faces with their shirts. Behind the burning tanker, the sunrise spreads its bloody light into the clouds, and the water undulates in shades of red and black. Everything is on fire. Not gay, not the quickened heart of adventure. The flames burn Sophie to her core, and she sees her girlish notions for what they were. Shame and fear turn her knees to ash. She kneels before the awful knowledge. War is a tunnel bored through the darkness. All of us riding blind, unsure what awaits us in the shadows until a flash reveals the faces of fiends.

The front door closes, and absence returns to apartment 2B. But there is still someone here to record the fact, this unseen eye that moves across the floor as if it were a page, sweeps the bedroom, the naked walls, lingers at the single living room window with its blinds at half-mast. The drop of white paint beside the bathtub, the polished and sterilized kitchen cabinets, the sanded floors that will still smell of pine two months from now, when the new tenants move in.

Four in the afternoon. Sounds fill the rooms. Listen: the complaint of old pipes, piano music that begins and stops and begins again, the tapping of thin branches on the windows, paint scraped on canvas, muffled voices through the walls, sometimes crying. Afternoon is ending, but the sunshine lingers, viscous and unsparing, the long day seeping into the corners of the apartment. Time, spooky and fickle. Not arrow, but snake.

EUGENIO, 1963

The great composer is dead. The news reaches Eugenio via his shortwave, the signal going in and out like a transmission from the beyond. Eugenio silences the radio and sits by the window, looking down at the street below. It cannot be. He was going to visit him after the new year. They had connected again, two old men now: their shame a historical artifact, lost along with everything else. It cannot be. Dead in Tenerife. Eugenio won't think of it. He won't accept it. It is not true. The regime playing its insidious games. After a while, he stands and begins to dust.

━━

Eugenio Francisco Montes Behar has lived in apartment 2B since 1952, the year of the coup. In Cuba, he was a famous concert pianist, but now he plays mostly weddings and a few local gigs: Friday and Saturday nights at the swanky Delano Hotel and Cabana Club down the street, and Sunday afternoons at an old person's home a block from the Tower Theater, in what some people are starting to call Little Havana. Eugenio himself never calls it that—those derelict streets full of barefoot vagabonds will never compare to his beloved Havana, with its colonnades and its parks, its grand gardens resplendent with palm and hibiscus.

Eugenio never planned to stay this long in apartment 2B, with its crooked bedroom door and the depression in the kitchen floor collecting grime. Maybe a few months, while he waited for Batista to be deposed—and now a decade has gone by just like that, with his hardly noticing, one despot replacing another. After the missile crisis, Eugenio understood that the waiting would continue, maybe even for another decade, so he hung a mezuzah by the bedroom door, the klaf encased in a simple silver case, in memory of his mother. And finally last year he started looking for land to buy. Si Dios quiere, next month he'll move into his own little house with its garden of overgrown bougainvillea.

He plans to stay in apartment 2B only until the closing. The new land is out west, at the end of the world, but it is all he can afford. He's determined not to die a renter. He may no longer be able to count on the Montes fortune, but neither is he impoverished. Anyway, his needs are modest: a house where he can install his grand piano—a real piano, not this secondhand upright—and play it whenever he wants. A house full of windows. A house in his future, even though Eugenio feels himself more and more pulled into the past. No matter how young we are when we abandon our country, the years grow heavy beneath us.

He is named after his father, the senior Eugenio Francisco Montes, who made his fortune as an art dealer and collector in the early days of the republic. Paintings covered every wall of their town house in El Vedado. Even the bathrooms had art—prints that his father would swap out every few months. There wasn't time to grow attached to the paintings. Most soon returned to the gallery or were sold. Eugenio never understood why some paintings hung in their house and others in the gallery. His sister Mercedes loved the paintings and from a young age could discuss the artists and the styles with a confidence that, to little Eugenio, at least, seemed genuine. But he never felt at ease amid so much static color. It was a kind of noise. Noise that became even more unbearable after his mother died the year Eugenio turned twelve. A few months after her death, Eugenio gathered the courage to ask his father to please remove every painting from his room. The elder Eugenio stood in the doorway, arms crossed. Sternly, his son thought. Then, to the boy's surprise, his father walked to the bed and hugged him. His father held him a long time, without words. For the rest of his life, Eugenio was not able to recall another instance of such tenderness. The touch, so warm and so unexpected, loosened months of emotion. Eugenio allowed himself to cry softly at first, and then, as Papá held him, to sob openly, deliciously, sobs that emerged round and heavy from the same secret place as the music.

His sweet and beautiful mother—Eugenio loved her with an intensity that has never diminished, ever, not a single bit.

It was from her that he learned his love of music, beginning with the sound of her voice. Years ago, a British journalist in Havana asked Eugenio when he knew he was going to be a musician. He was asked this often. But this time Eugenio answered without his usual deliberation, without the need to sound intelligent. "Hearing my mother's voice," he said. "More precisely her Spanish." Eugenio believed that hearing Spanish from an early age primed him for music. A ridiculous assertion. Every language shapes its great artists. But for Eugenio, there was something in the Spanish that taught him melody before he could even speak. It was the Spanish language, as much as his mother's piano, that made him a musician. She had given a few concerts in her teens. And even after she gave up performing, music remained a source of joy she transmitted to her son. Music for her was not merely the melody that entered the ears. It was a solid thing with form and texture. And many times, after Eugenio finished practicing a piece, she closed her eyes and said, "Good, but the first movement should be more porous." Or, praising a performance of Bach, she said, "You hear that second variation, how it is just a bit more pebbly than the first?" Mozart was butter softening by the stove. Rachmaninoff was weathered wood, exposed nails. Eugenio never heard music the way his mother did—for her it was intuitive, some extra sense she had been born with, like those rare people who can see more of the color spectrum. But he spent enough of his boyhood at her side to appreciate that there was this other way to experience the notes. And with practice, he was able to approximate it. A kind of cheating, of course, but for his mother's sake, he trained himself to feel music as if it were solid material beneath his fingertips.

Mamá was an exuberant woman, and Eugenio saw her cry just once. She was at the piano playing something new. Usually she played Chopin or Mozart—his father's favorites. But this afternoon she played a melody that seemed to come out of her being, one in harmony with whatever secrets she kept inside. Eugenio listened, and when, some moments into the playing, his mother's shoulders started to shake, he was so moved that he cried out. His mother turned suddenly, her face stained with tears. Eugenio ran to her, and she held him. "Niño mio," she murmured into his hair. She let him sit next to her as she took up the music again. Eugenio has not forgotten any of this. One does not forget one's first Mahler. They sat together as she played the piece again, and then a third time. Now and then the boy glanced at her . . . Sitting straight in her chair, eyes opened, an expression he didn't recognize but that he associated with the unfathomable world of adults. The notes spoke eloquently and effortlessly of a sadness without measure. And yet, something beautiful in the wilderness of that sorrow, some feeling that rose and fell within him, incomprehensible, and yet complete. He knew something was being transmitted that would forever mark the frontier between the boy he was and the man he was becoming.

"Mahler understood morriña," his mother told him. "The wandering, the illusion that completion and return is at hand, that is what gives a work meaning. And here's a secret, mi niño, one you'll discover soon enough: the suspicion that one will never return, that the past will never be recovered, is part of the indescribable pleasure of morriña."

This was a year before his mother's death. Maybe his mother had tried to prepare him that afternoon. But Eugenio could not accept that the dead vanish forever. Even now, the memory brought him fresh pain. We trail our pasts like a dragon's tail, Eugenio decided, wondering now and then at its destructive beauty. But with time, he came to see that the dark variations within a piece, the unexpected tonal shifts, the frustrated end, derive their sublime force from the bright opening and the normal human desire for completion. Now he understands why his mother transcribed the symphony for piano: completion remains the specter beyond the last note.

WAS IT THE MUSIC, THEN, OR THE MAN THAT HE fell in love with? The composer would never claim to be the equal of Mahler. But in Eugenio's mind, the two became one. Eugenio searches now through the albums on the shelf until he finds it. He hasn't played it in years. Summoning all the delicacy of touch that his mother taught him, Eugenio lifts the needle, letting it gently meet the slick outer band. First the dull sound of metal caressing the groove guard, and then, like an apparition, the quivering first notes stitching themselves together. The fabric of sound envelopes him, not a shroud, no, no: a curtain, the curtain that fluttered one afternoon in the window of their rented room in Vigo where the composer would perform later that night. The curtain expanding in and out with sound: the low bass of ship horns off the harbor, the mocking cackle of seagulls, the comparsa of laughter in the street below, and then, in a moment that stopped time, the sonorous peal of church bells ringing, still ringing to this day.

MORRIÑA . . . MORRIÑA IS AN OLD MAN IN A RED shirt. It is the beauty inside sadness . . . there's no meaning in it and no understanding, either. Don't try. Morriña was listening to his mother play Mahler. "The Second Symphony," she told him that day, "is about the whole world." And she didn't try to hide her tears. It was a kind of gift.

Morriña is an old, old man at the nursing home where Eugenio plays on Sundays. The man always waits for him, calls him El Músico. He stands by the piano, thin legs squeezed together, his large hands hugging the side of his thighs. He always wears the same denim shirt, tucked into a pair of high-waisted corduroys. His hair is still thick and plentiful. His eyebrows nearly obscure his eyes, which turn down at the corners. His teeth sit large and yellow in his half-opened mouth. His thin shoulders are always slightly bent. The others call him Bobo—the old are every bit as cruel as children. Eugenio cannot be sure how much he understands of their teasing. The old man never reacts to it. He reacts only to the music.

Late that night, with no concern for the neighbors, Eugenio sits at the upright, playing from memory. He reaches for the familiar notes without thought, as if the other's hands guided his own fingers, grown cold. La Malagueña sends her regrets. Melancolía wrests Lola from the party. The notes swell and expand the apartment walls like a bell. All of it returns to him, distorted in convex: the cry of ship horns, the self-hating seagulls, the comparsa of shame. Laughter is hereby outlawed. Close the music box and shatter the crystal doll. Dress Maria de la O in her mourning cloak—the great Lecuona is dead!

The apartment is empty now. The indentation in the kitchen floor sags a little deeper; water rattles in the pipes. The last tenant left the windows opened a crack and the curtains dance and sing. Perhaps it is their movement that gives the illusion that someone is still walking up here, slowly pacing the length of the small room, wearing the Florida pine floors, little by little exposing the grain.

SANDMAN, 1972

Head on fire, Sandman wakes in an unfamiliar room. The sound of choppers overhead. Lights crisscross the darkness. He closes his eyes. When he opens them again, it is morning, and he remembers where he is. He lifts himself slowly from the narrow bed. Apartment 2B: "Home" these last seven months. The pad was supposed to be furnished, but when he arrived with his one duffel bag, all he found was the aluminum-frame bed in one of the bedrooms and a termite-eaten credenza in the other. A tangle of wire hangers in the big closet. The living room had no sofa, just a reclining chair covered in a hideous flower pattern, the life gone out of it long ago. At least there was a pine table in the small dining room, with one chair where he could sit every morning with his coffee and curse his new life, where the only thing to look forward to is the mail.

In the kitchen, spent bottles of Jim Beam line the stove. Empty Schlitz cans sit in a bucket under the sink, and at night the roaches rattle through them, as desperate for their sweet solace as is Sandman. Seventy-one dollars a month, a rip-off for this dump. But you don't look a gift horse in the mouth, even when it's from your wife, your ex-wife, though he refuses to accept that, the ex part. What kind of woman divorces her man while he's drowning? A real bitch. But she found him this place. True, it's as far away from her and the kid as she could manage. *Until you can get back on your feet.* The thing is: She wouldn't really want him out of her life if she's still helping him, right? She'll give him a year, she said. Then she stops paying. Sandman's pretty sure that's what he heard. It was the first and last time they spoke on the phone. Sandman sweating inside the booth on Washington that always stank of cigarettes. Feeding it nickels and quarters, searching his pockets for a few more seconds of her voice. Yeah, yeah, sweetheart. One year and I'm coming home, your mommy and daddy can stop paying for their worthless son-in-law.

In that first phone call, she made a big deal about the whole thing: the cost, the furniture, and, especially, the brand-new Carrier stuck in the living room window like a stone in the throat. An air conditioner! What a stupid idea—must have been his mother-in-law's. Sandman will never turn it on. Hell, these days he can't sleep unless the mosquitoes are joyriding off his skin. Sandman said yeah, yeah, and then asked about the kid. It's cool, she said, *all groovy,* as if she were still a teenager.

Now he remembers the choppers. Another goddamn protest, probably. Some silk-palmed doves carrying placards. Baby killer, that wasn't him. Not babies. He thought that when he abandoned the war for good, he'd find some rest. But the whole goddamn world was on fire. At night, the strange presence that hovers over his bed, threatening to smother him. And the morning after, the weight of whiskey migraines. He'd left a country stuck in the bedrock and returned to one floating on lava. And he was the volcano. Time coils around him. Flamingo Park suddenly appearing in the guise of his old Catholic school carnivals, every freak with his own booth. Sandman gone so long he doesn't know the fucking difference between a Zippie and a Yippie. Whose idea was it to line a path in chalk and call it the Ho Chi Minh Trail? Bad community theater is what it is, full of performers without the balls to sit in the jungle and listen for the deadly variations in the buzzing. Yesterday, he found the tent with the display on Vietnam: *Expose '72*. Bunch of strung-out commies. I'll show you expose. But hardly anyone noticed when he lowered his pants and mooned the lot of them. One hippie girl actually clapped. Fuck, man, now he'd become part of the entertainment in this cheap carnival town.

He pours some cornflakes in a bowl. The milk is going sour. At eleven, he grabs his wallet and the slip of paper and heads to the post office. About once a month, his wife sends him a package, something that belonged to him in that old life. The first time it happened, he panicked to find a slip in the mailbox directing him to come down to the post office. Poured out a cup of whiskey to settle himself before he saw the name of the sender. That time it was a box of books, the stuff he used to read back in the day: Jack London, James Michener. Just looking at the purple cover of *Tales of the South Pacific* fills Sandman with longing, even after he's been close enough to know better. There was a small note on the top of that first box of books, *I thought you'd be missing these.* Unsigned, but her handwriting, of course. He lined the books along the dusty baseboards. The note he taped above his bed. The next time it was his All-American trophy, tight end, 1968. It sits now on the pine table, collecting pennies. The note that time read simply: *Something to be proud of.* The next package contained his coffee cup and the four silver place settings he inherited from his grandmother. There was no note with that package or the ones that followed: his coin collection, a photograph of his parents, his dress shoes—black, size eleven, Florsheims (he bought them for the wedding and never wore them again, having shipped out five months later, his wife just beginning to show); his high school football jersey (#23) and the striped sweater she knit for him as a graduation gift; a lava lamp she bought as a joke. Slowly the objects took up residence in the place, as if the apartment itself were a living thing, lighting up with memories.

Sandman started accumulating so much old junk that he needed a place to put it. One night, on a half-drunken walk through the alleys, he found an abandoned pile of wooden pallets. He hauled them to the apartment and nailed together a low set of shelves. There, he installed the books that had been collecting dust on the floor. Another night, he found a wooden stool, feet up in a Dumpster. He would have to climb in to grab it, and he hesitated. He knew what he must look like: long-haired skinny freak, fucked-up vet in his American flag T-shirt. But he took it home, washing it in the tub as if it were a newborn. That week, he walked down to Ace and begged for a sheet of sandpaper. The guy at the counter, also a vet, threw in a half-empty can of varnish. Now the stool sat by the door, a place to keep his wallet and his keys, all of it watched over by the nonfunctioning phone stuck to the wall.

The post office is on Thirteenth and Washington. The first time he walked there, he was overwhelmed: The car engines backfiring, all the honking, the people shouting. Light through the palm blades, the jungle buzz. Even the laughter of children made him jump. He had to close his eyes and stop every few blocks. It was better at night, when he could roam under cover of darkness, the city muted. But slowly he was able to walk farther and farther without stopping. He noticed things now: The light coming off the chrome bumper of the red Mustang always parked at the corner of Eleventh and Euclid. The neon sign over Sol's that flickered when storm clouds darkened the facade.

Today, the sound of distant marchers somewhere on Washington. Voices that ebb and flow like ocean waves until he is surrounded by the cacophony. Sandman flattens himself against a coconut palm. A line of protesters pass him, carrying a Cuban flag and shouting something in Spanish. At the post office, the fans are blowing like mad. Sandman hangs on to his paper—he'd lost his slip once and nearly punched the dude who put his foot on it. Today, he waits in line behind an old lady with a scarf over her hair. She moves so slowly that Sandman must resist the urge to shove her along. Or just pick her up and deposit her in front of the window already. Finally, it's his turn. The girl is a looker; he's seen her before. A hippie type with long hair parted on either side of her face. This is probably her summer job, a way to make a little extra dough between semesters.

"Hi, baby," he says.

The girl frowns and takes the slip without looking at him. She disappears behind the wooden partitions and returns with a box that is only a little bigger than the shoebox his wife mailed him last month.

"Thank you, baby."

"Next," the girl says.

Sandman holds the box. It's very light, the lightest box his ex-wife has ever sent. He shakes it. A slight rattle.

Back in the apartment, he opens the box with his field knife . . . He lifts the flaps and stares inside, not believing. Empty. Empty-empty, as in nothing in it, no shredded newspapers, no note. Checking the front, he sees that this package has no return address, either. Just his own name written in his wife's—ex-wife's—perfect Palmer script. What the fuck? Someone nab what was in it? He picks up the phone on the wall before remembering the line hasn't been connected yet. Goddamn bureaucracy. He returns the dead receiver to its cradle. No one stole shit. She meant to send him an empty box. What the hell was this supposed to mean? Who would go through the trouble of sending an empty box? He pours himself a mugful and then another. He sleeps.

Twilight wakes him, again the sound of choppers. Through the open windows, the smell of something burning. He knocks back the trickle of whiskey left in the mug, just to set his head right, and grabs his keys. Over the low buildings, smoke rising from the area of Flamingo Park. At the booth, he turns the numbers, calling collect. She refuses the call. He slams the phone down and a few moments later rattles in his pockets for change. Feeds the nickels into the machine, tries again. She doesn't pick up. He tries three more times. A line has begun to form outside. He walks out of the booth and stops, stunned for a moment by the orange sky. The smoke has magnified the sunset and now everything is bathed in other-planetary light: the trees, the sidewalk, his own hands. Knees weak, Sandman begins to walk back to the apartment.

More choppers overhead. Something about the way the blades reflect the fading light. This goddamn humidity. Sandman turns onto Eleventh, looking for a place to catch his breath. His hands tingle, and he feels hollow. As if those last medics had taken out his insides, cleaned him out. Something off with his brain—he knows this—brain not connected quite right. The vision off. He follows a sound. From the direction of Flamingo Park an army marches toward him. An army of ashen-faced zombies. Dozens of them. Sandman reaches for his rifle, comes up empty. Behind the pale soldiers, a platoon of Nixons, faces smeared with blood. As they get closer, Sandman can make out what they're shouting. *One, two, three, four, we don't want your fucking war.* He's confused at first. Thinking they're addressing him personally. Not my war, not my war! And then it's all fucking hilarious. Sandman laughs as the procession streams past him. *One, two, three, four, I don't want my fucking war!* And now the sound of glass breaking. Sandman turns. Across the street, a man in a SMASH THE STATE T-shirt smashes a police car with a baseball bat. Another hooligan throws a piece of concrete through an apartment window. Around the corner sprints a man, with another one on his heels. And suddenly the street is full of freaks chasing one another. Fuck, man, don't call me bent. Whole country has lost its goddamn mind. Police sirens scream down the street, and Sandman runs in the opposite direction.

The sun is setting. The beach is deserted except for a couple huddled on the sand, and a bearded man passed out next to his shopping bag. When the wind shifts from the west, Sandman can hear the protesters' self-satisfied roars. But here, on the sand, a strange calm, a waiting. Sandman approaches the ocean's edge, the world shifting, reality fracturing beneath him. He is overcome with a sudden urge—a command!—to jump into the waves. Near the end of his final tour, he understood that the world was barely held together, and if you looked closely enough, you could see the cracks. The world was nothing but an improvised rig! The insight felt so real that he couldn't keep it to himself. He'd said it out loud too many times. Honorable discharge. *Honorable.* Hell, yeah, man! Didn't get more honorable than this: Him cracking open alongside the world, one of the chosen, a specially chosen fuckup. Walking behind his buddies suddenly seeing that same orange sky, the illumination. Aware—no, certain—that he was, that they all were, characters in a made-up world. These branches, this mud, the mosquitoes, all bullshit! This fear, a mirage; the void inside him just the edge of the great void surrounding them all.

The only thing left to do is walk into the ocean to repair the cracks. Night falls suddenly. The ocean calls his name, his real name, which he has never shared with anyone except Uncle Sam. The ocean knows him. A sliver of moon rises over the water and illuminates the shadows all around him. The sliver grows, expanding like a belly, until it ruptures, dripping light on the waves. Tiny shadows encircle him: creatures. Sandman stands very still as they emerge from the depths beneath the sand, hundreds of them. For a moment Sandman is not sure what he is seeing. This must be another vision. He steps back from the water. The creatures surround him. Sandman bends. He'll be damned: tiny turtles running away, running toward their looming moon shadows, toward the even brighter lights of the city.

He shakes his head. None of this is real, man.

He turns back to the sea; a highway illuminates his path straight to the moon. All he is called to do now is follow it. He steps into the water. Another step. Deeper, the water to his waist. To his neck. To his chin. He tastes the salt. And suddenly Sandman stops. He begins to laugh and his mouth fills with the sea. The absurdity at the heart of life! That's it!

It suddenly strikes him: Life is neither tragic nor joyful, it is absurd! It's hilarious! He is walking toward the turtles' destiny, and they are walking toward his—and all of them will die for no reason.

He turns back to the sand.

"No, no!" he shouts after the turtles. "Not that way, morons!"

Sandman runs after the creatures. He picks up two of them and runs back to the shore. Returns, picks up two more. But the turtles now are streaming like the possessed, away from the water. "You want to be crushed? What's the matter with you?" He stretches out his American flag T-shirt and fills it with squirming baby turtles. Runs to the water's edge and back again for more. The couple huddled on the sand see him and empty out their cooler. As fast as they can, the three of them fill the cooler with the fugitives and drop them into the ocean. More people join them. The passed-out man rouses himself and offers his battered Richard's bag. Someone else brings a packing crate. They work for almost an hour, Sandman and these strangers, returning the turtles to the sea. They throw them in and watch as they swim away, enchanted travelers on that luminous highway.

Sandman smiles. He holds the last turtle in his hands.

"It's all a fiction, baby. None of this is real." He opens his hands and listens for the splash. The water moves away from the creature in concentric circles.

"All the same, you dumb fuck," he shouts, "this is where you belong."

*Pepe and Chucho are painting the interior walls of apartment 2B,
and Pepe is teasing Chucho about his operation earlier this year.*

*It sounds like the setup for a Cuban joke, but those are their real
nicknames, used for so long that they've half forgotten each other's
given names.*

"I heard the head nurse had a beard,"

"That's right," Chucho says. "And she smoked a cigar."

*Pepe laughs, dips the roller in the tray of white paint, paints
another stripe onto the walls of apartment 2B.*

*"Sin jodér, I think the old son of a bitch was there at the same
time," Chucho says. "You wouldn't believe the security. It was like
a state visit."*

*Pepe shakes his head. "Everyone makes the best decision he can,
but I would never have gone."*

*Chucho puts his roller down and stretches. "What choice did I
have? I got to where I couldn't walk two steps. Do you have any
idea how much knee surgery costs here?"*

*"It didn't used to be like that. This country used to have the best
health care system in the world. And then we got a peanut farmer
for president. Before you know it, we'll all be traveling to China
for operations."*

*Chucho shrugs. "It's not like I gave money to the Commu-
nists. It was my cousin's son who did the operation. It stays in
the family."*

"Still," Pepe says. "I wouldn't go around here saying you traveled to Cuba for medical care."

"*Dios me libre!*" Chucho says. "Still, look at me. I have the knees of a teenager again. This last weekend, I was able to take the grandkids to the new zoo."

"That's the difference between you and me," Pepe says. "If I were a teenager again, the zoo would not be the first place I'd go to celebrate."

Chucho laughs. Another dip in the paint, another stripe. "How is Sara?"

"Sara! My brilliant son-in-law just got himself fired from Publix," says Pepe.

"Again?"

"No, the last one was Jordan Marsh."

"Ah. At least Sarita has her career."

"All thanks to her mother," Pepe says. "Nidia always told her to not count on men. Used to bother me—what the hell was I? But then I accepted that they hadn't really been able to count on me, either, so it was fair."

"Well, my friend, we caught an unlucky break, that's all," Chucho says.

"*No jodas,*" Pepe says. "And today a bunch of sons-of-barbudos are sailing around in your yacht while you get surgery down the street."

Chucho says, "Tralala." Pepe laughs. They take up the rollers again.

"What's this aluminum thing here by the door?"

Pepe inspects the case, its delicate carvings. "No idea."

"Should we remove it?"

"Nah. Just paint over it."

And then for about an hour there is only the sound of the rollers, the thick slopping of paint.

"The best part was the apes," Chucho says after a long silence.

"What are you talking about?"

"The apes—at Metro Zoo. I told you, we went this past weekend."

"It sounds like a pain in the ass."

"It's hot," Chucho says. "But we walked everywhere, and my knees were excellent."

"And the apes?"

"They let them roam around. Without cages. And they had this little setup with a big watering hole. Most of the orangutans, or whatever they were, were resting in the shade, because of the heat, I figure. But there was one, a small skinny one, who went down to the watering hole and was drinking. This was a big water hole, maybe half an acre around, room for everyone. But a big ape saw him. He waited long enough for the skinny little ape to feel comfortable. The son of a bitch waited for him to drink for a while, and then you know what he did?"

"He popped open a beer."

"No, imbecile. He walked down to the water hole, in no hurry, really, and got up right beside the smaller ape and shoved him so hard, he nearly fell in. Then the big ape bent down to drink from that very same spot. As if it were the only place in the world that he could drink."

"I think I've seen that guy driving on the Palmetto," Pepe says.

"*That's my point,*" Chucho says. "*If you want to understand people, go watch the apes.*"

The men paint in silence for a while.

"*Is that it for the first coat?*" Chucho says after a while.

"*Pretty much.*"

"*Let's eat, then. We can paint the grilles after lunch and do the second coat tomorrow morning.*"

"*Where do we wash these things? Is there a hose down there?*" Pepe asks.

"*What the hell, the stairs are a mother. Let's just wash them right here in the tub.*"

ISABEL, 1982

She should be grateful, but Isabel hates the apartment. Miami Beach! In Cuba, the name dripped with cachet. Isabel imagined streets lined with convertibles and glamorous couples drinking daiquiris in view of the sea. Instead here she is, a secret guest in her lover's crummy art studio. Probably he chose it for the small kitchen with the door that conveniently opens to the back alley. Never mind the floor sinking in the middle. The main bedroom has a closet where he keeps his paints. The smaller bedroom holds a futon, for those nights when he gets caught up in the work. One small disgusting bathroom, its washbasin and bathtub stained with paint. The rest of the apartment, the part that might have been the "living" area in a normal home, was a purgatory of half-completed paintings and spent paint tubes, the wood floor speckled beyond the boundaries of the wrinkled canvases that never quite cover the surface.

So Isabel escapes every chance she gets. She had been such a cautious little girl. But that first escape from Cuba, terrifying as it was, primed her. Nothing bad happens from leaving, she decided, only from staying. And even though South Beach is almost as run-down as Havana, Isabel loves the night. Loves the languid, emptied feel of the city after dark. As she walks, she imagines herself complicit with the cataclysmic vapors that hang about the gutters, rustle in the high branches. From the second story of the Helena, the abandoned streets seem grave-silent except for the occasional screams of seagulls, the sirens of distant emergencies. But Isabel believes she is unsentimental, not one to make scenes or dissolve in self-pity. She savors her aimless meanderings along Meridian Avenue under its lush canopy, to Lincoln Road to look at the Judaica shops, and then down to the ocean to take in the derelict Delano Hotel, the boarded-up windows, the paint chipping on those enormous rooftop fins. All these excursions into the ruins are less a running away than a guiding to, she tells herself. Strolling to her next life. She just turned eighteen and is in no hurry.

———

She stands by herself.

"Are you open?"

Jacobo remembers her: a beauty amid the vagrants and pimps of Washington Avenue. For the last few months, she's been coming in with the artist. The girl—for she can't be much older than twenty—always hangs from the man's elbow, imitating some borrowed image of this sort of thing. They came in last week. The artist did not ignore Jacobo, but neither did he linger, as he sometimes did. They left before the coffee. Jacobo is neither painter nor poet, and in the girl's slender gesture he didn't see romance, only the spectacle of an orchid clinging to a ruined oak.

Now Jacobo sweeps his right hand across the empty terrace. "Of course. Sit anywhere you like." The girl chooses a table out on the sidewalk and sits facing the street, her back to the restaurant. Jacobo cradles two menus but doesn't move to deliver them. He stands at the doorway, watching the girl. Her black hair fans glossy across bare shoulders. She doesn't turn around. She's not one of the impatient ones; that's probably what the artist likes about her. One of the things. After a moment, she reaches into her bag and, shoulders rising in a sigh, opens a book and settles back in her chair.

════

"Ahora se anunciaba un gran baile de pastores—de estilo ya muy envejecido en París." Isabel removed the book from the shelf that morning, after he'd gone home. He teased her the night before about never having read Carpentier. He teased her like this, now and then, and it was fine. Because it was no slur to say she was a Marielita, no fault of hers that her education halted the moment they boarded an old fishing vessel with its funny name, *Oh, Calcutta!* How Miguel laughed at her incomprehension. Miguel, who went by *Michel* now, ever since signing with the New York gallery, but still Mickey to his old friends, her father remaining one of them, not knowing any better. Miguel kept apartment 2B as a second studio—or so

Isabel figured he told his wife. It wasn't a total lie: He did paint there. Isabel first sat for him almost a year ago, every Thursday afternoon for a month, lying on a cloth-covered sofa, one long arm grazing the floor. And after the last session, when he finished consuming her image and digested it onto the canvas, Michel led her to the futon. He enjoyed her inside and out, slowly, exquisitely, and it was there, at the slope of pleasure, where she grew full and buoyant for the first time—felt, yes, this was all she needed to know in this life.

It was not her first sexual experience. But she doubted now whether she could consider those furtive penetrations of her girlhood *experiences* at all, for Miguel did not just enter her body. He took possession of her being, and even a passing thought of him was enough to transform her into a pulsating beam penetrating the emptiness between galaxies, a thing of pure searching. He was much older, and she loved him, though she would never say that to anyone. She could well see how they looked from the outside, their terribly commonplace situation. More shameful in its lack of originality than in its betrayals. And though she wanted to be a writer, she knew she would never write about this.

She did not plan on moving into his studio. It was not the reason she told him of another beating at the hands of his old friend from the institute. Mickey knew her father was a drunk. And maybe he took pity, or maybe something else already contaminated that pure emotion. But he made a set of keys for her. She could stay a few weeks until she found work, he said. In the meantime, if someone in the building were to ask who she was, she was to respond, "The cleaning lady." Isabel saw no shame in that, either. And anyway, no one ever did ask. He stayed overnight at least once a week, always leaving her money in the morning for that week's groceries, a little extra for herself. He told her never to walk alone at night, a warning that Isabel ignored whenever she could.

She reads now in front of the battered diner where Miguel had brought her so many times, turning pages in a suspended state induced by Carpentier's opaque prose. Already she's had to stop and reread the same passage over and over: Monsieur Lenormand de Mezy returns to marry the rich widow again and again—still limping, still devoted—until Isabel puts the book down and signals to the waiter.

He nods, approaching. "Señorita." He lays down two menus, which Isabel ignores. She looks up at him, remembering to make eye contact, as Miguel taught her.

"Please, a steak and french fries."

"¿Bistec y papitas fritas, algo más?"

Isabel pauses. "And a glass of wine."

"Tinto?"

"Red, yes, thank you." Isabel speaks English everywhere. It's the only way to learn it, Miguel says. They even speak it when they are alone, in the most intimate moments.

The waiter purses his lips. "Está bien."

=====

Marielita, Jacobo decides. He fills the wineglass, and the girl mumbles a "Thanks" from the depths of her book. He relays her order to Sam and waits for him to fry the steak and potatoes in his obsessive and unnecessarily baroque style. Sam fired the cook last week—drugs, or, to be more precise, money stolen for—and Sam has taken over the kitchen. He is very slow. But still a surprisingly good cook for all his sour cursing. And slow doesn't matter when there are hardly any customers. Business has been steadily dropping for two years now, riots, invasions, you name it, all the plagues. Jacobo is close to retirement. What does it matter to him? He leans against the doorway to wait, looking out over the terrace. It's not even dark yet, but it's possible that the girl will be the only customer today. Even Jacobo urged Sam to sell the place, cash out while he could. But the man was as stubborn as he was mean, two qualities that only hardened after his wife's death that past spring. Jacobo allowed Sam to go on thinking that he feared and hated him. But he heard the old goat sobbing one night behind the moth-eaten curtain of his office. Jacobo has not been able to forget the sound, how lonely it was. He was never religious, but a fragment from a childhood service returned to him then . . . *'tis a fearful thing to love what death can touch* . . . What a strange and hopeful animal man was. To love as if loss existed for others and never for us. To yearn as if time were forever. We are all like this girl with her married lover, Jacobo thinks. Strolling blind through our graveyards, slender limbs entwined.

═══

"Voilà." The waiter sets down her food. The steak flops over the edges of the plate. The whole thing covered with a mound of thin fries. Isabel thanks the waiter, and he gives a slight bow.

"Some more wine?" The waiter lifts the bottle.

"Please, thank you."

The waiter tilts his head in a half nod and pours.

Isabel puts the book down, splayed open so she doesn't lose the page. She chews slowly. After a moment, she notices someone moving across the street, in front of the boarded storefront. Her heart leaps—Miguel! But it couldn't be. She knows that tonight he has an official engagement—with his official family. Perhaps, though, he has stolen away to see her. Not finding her at home, he'd know where she was, even though he'd be angry with her. He warned her not to leave the house without him. The streets weren't safe for anyone in this part of the beach, much less a young woman. Two nights ago, a woman was raped at Flamingo Park. The week previous, a man was shot dead a block from the apartment. Last month, a friend of Michel's was stabbed three times in the thigh in a robbery outside Joe's Stone Crabs. "These aren't anecdotes," Miguel said, angry, as if this were all her doing, which maybe he thought it was. "Nonsense," she said. "I'm perfectly safe with you or without you. All of these warnings are just a way to keep women down, to keep us locked up indoors."

Miguel suddenly grew pale. He balled his fists "¡No seas imbécil!" he shouted, forgetting, in his heat, the injunction against Spanish: "La playa se ha llenado de escoria. You're not safe, you little idiot."

That last part stung. But Isabel smiled through it.

"Okay, papito, no te preocupes," she said. "I'll stay in. Don't worry."

He took a deep breath and reached out to caress her hair. "It's not safe for a young woman," he said. "I care about you." He appeared to calm down. But later, as he tied his shoes, he did so roughly. And it seemed to Isabel that his manner toward her had cooled.

THE FIGURE PACING BACK AND FORTH IN FRONT OF the boarded window now crosses the street, looking in Isabel's direction. Isabel stops chewing. She keeps her eyes on him. The figure approaches and Isabel's heart constricts with fear. It is not Miguel. A stranger. But as the person comes closer, Isabel relaxes. Her nerves restored, she even gives a small laugh. Not Miguel, not a man at all: Close enough to smell now, the skulking figures reveals itself to be an old woman. She is slightly bent and carries a battered paper bag. Her once-dark hair hangs like a dirty fringe over her shoulders, and she's dressed unusually warm for the night in a green army coat. She passes, and Isabel looks down into her food. It is a lovely evening, really. Tropical winter. The sky still has some light in it. It's unusually still. Isabel turns and notices for the first time that she is the only patron in the restaurant. No wonder the waiter is in such a miserable mood. Isabel spears two fries and chews them slowly.

The night, the wine, the warm food. Isabel returns to the memory of that morning, Miguel entering her at last, a second orgasm, sharp on the edge of self and desire and if—but Isabel is confused now. Seeing Miguel again above her, but not Miguel, the old woman in the army coat. The old woman with her hands on Isabel's plate. Isabel's first impulse is to grab the plate back from her with a force that launches a spray of fries over the sidewalk. Mine, mine! Isabel cries.

Suddenly the waiter is on them, shouting so fast that Isabel cannot understand what he's saying. The woman spits on his shoes and then bends to gather the fallen french fries as fast as she's able, stuffing them into the pockets of her coat as she crawls along the sidewalk. "Shoo, shoo!" The waiter chases her off the floor and across the street, waving and clapping his hands. When she reaches the opposite curb, the woman turns around. "Fuck you!" she shouts. Then she takes a fry from her pocket and smiles at Isabel. Isabel will never forget that smile. I know you, the smile says. I see you. The waiter turns to Isabel and sucks his teeth. He grabs the plate from Isabel's hands and, muttering complaints, whisks it away.

For the second time tonight, someone has snatched Isabel's plate from her. What is she being punished for? It wasn't her fault, was it? The woman swooped in out of nowhere with her terrifying want, her bony hands. What could Isabel have done?

======

Sam is not in the kitchen. Jacobo calls out to him. "Druggies and pimps," Jacobo shouts. "That's who we serve now. I know you're back there, but you can't hide behind your feeble curtain! The whole city is a cesspool, and you insist on keeping this dump open, for what? So that playboys can bring their secret playthings. So they won't have to answer to colleagues, all of them smugly safe in the Gables."

Jacobo mutters as he moves around the kitchen. "And we are here with the garbage in the streets!"

The girl would probably leave without paying, so be it. Twenty years working for Sam. Twenty winters. Twenty hurricane seasons. Riots. Boatlifts. How he used to look forward to winters, those years when the sidewalks still filled. He grabs a steak from the freezer, starts up the oil. There is no real beauty in this world except what we make for ourselves.

Isabel sits at her empty table, her wine gone. The book like a squashed bug beside her. It has all gone badly, hasn't it? It stings to think what Miguel would make of the scene. Well. She should wait for the check and pay it and walk back to the studio, and she wouldn't say a word of it to Miguel, ever. He'd never know she defied him, that she dined by herself and that her dinner was stolen twice.

She thought of the old woman. The gray fringe of hair across her back. She reminded her of someone. Another woman, perhaps, not herself. How many women did Miguel have? How many did he keep in other studios? He admired Picasso, said that anyone who wasn't an artist could not understand that the drive to create something out of nothing was the very definition of the sexual act. Without sex and desire there would be no art. No eunuch ever created a symphony, my pretty one. Art, he said, grabbing his genitals, art comes from here. About his own wife, he never spoke. One afternoon, Isabel asked too many questions and he handled her roughly. He left a mark on her wrist. That night, alone in the studio, Isabel heard the crying for the first time, which stopped her heart: it seemed to be coming from the room where Miguel stored his blank canvases. The glowing red numbers on the digital clock were hard to read. Was it three in the morning? Isabel kept very still in the bed, listening. After a moment, she rose from the futon. Miguel never installed curtains and now the streetlamps lit up the apartment, casting long shadows over the half-completed paintings. Robbed of color in the darkness, the canvases all seemed to depict graveyard scenes. Isabel lingered outside the bedroom. A rustling. Then something knocked over a canvas. Isabel stopped dead, sirens flooding her ears.

"Mice," Miguel told her the next time he visited. He showed her the droppings.

Mice, then. There were rational explanations. She was a Marielita from a countryside populated by ghosts, trying to pass in the exile's rational world. But she had felt it: the presence that tried to stop her lungs at night.

THE WAITER REAPPEARS. BUT, TO ISABEL'S astonishment, instead of the check, he carries a new plate, freshly replenished, as if the first had not been consumed or defiled. As if the old woman had been an illusion, or a visitation from a future whose branch just died here, on a trash-strewn street in South Beach, 1982. The night rewinds, the canvas reverts to white, and Isabel has only just arrived at the diner, alone with her hunger. The waiter drops the platter in front of her. Isabel looks up, but before she can speak, he points his finger in her face and growls, "¡Presta atención!"

MARGOT, 1984

The first thing her husband did when they walked into apartment 2B was crush a white mouse that skittered across the wood floor. Margot Benini brought her manicured hands to her mouth and let out a scream.

"For heaven's sake, Margot, keep quiet," her husband said.

Mrs. Benini composed herself. She adjusted her coiffure, which she wore swept back high like a spun-sugar crown, though she was only twenty-seven years old that summer.

"You've ruined your shoes," she said.

HER LAST NAME HAS BEEN CHANGED—THE PASsive voice is intentional, as she herself has not been apprised of who did the changing—but it is similar enough to the old secret name that she seems only a partial stranger to herself. Anyway, the old name wasn't her name, it was her husband's name, though it was one she liked, and now and then, in this new place, she grows sad for the vanished life that the name symbolized. But her husband promised apartment 2B is only a stopping point, while things are worked out, details—again, by whom she wasn't informed. Good people have given them refuge in the U.S., that's all she knows. And here they are, Margot Benini and her husband Martin from Uruguay because the accent better matches the place they are really from, and Miami is a place that notices accents.

Later, Margot will acknowledge that in her old life, when she lived above the famous street in the apartment her parents gifted her and her new husband, she was ignorant about almost everything. She knew nothing about her parents' role in society and certainly nothing about her new husband's place in the terror slowly engulfing their country. And now, in 1984, newly arrived at the Helena, Margot remains ignorant—she doesn't even know enough about the world to know that she doesn't know. It was a shock—the news they were leaving. And so abrupt. An overnight flight to an unknown country— they even kept that from her. Then another flight. Two days in an apartment in the hills of some island—she could smell the sea, even with the windows closed. And now dropped in Miami Beach, where her husband has work to do. In the English novels she studied in school, the characters all seemed masters of their own fates. When they stumbled, it was because of a flaw. The direction their lives took was the direction they determined through their choices. But this was not Margot's experience of the world. The world so far acted on her without consultation or sympathy. Her life, dictated first by her parents' wealth and now by her husband's work, lacked the agency she was taught to recognize in great works. Even this latest leaving had been out of her hands. Maybe the only true literature was the old ghost stories her grandmother used to whisper to her on those windy cold nights on the Pampas. Spirit and mortals alike, all subject to unseen forces that swelled beneath them, hidden and untamable.

=====

She'd been allowed only one suitcase, and this had been pawed over by every security dog they'd come across. What were they looking for? Always, they left her silks in a sad pile. How she cried those two days in the apartment in the hills—the shabbiness of it, the single toilet with a flush chain, the windows that rattled in the incessant wind. And now this, this was even worse: an apartment the size of a horse stable, two cramped bedrooms, a single toilet. A kitchen no bigger than a closet, and less useful. Decorated in the most utilitarian style, with uninspiring brown furniture. Everything in the rooms seemed to scream, *Blend in!*, as if their handlers—whoever they were—thought they could send subliminal reminders to them. In B.—in the old place—she felt vibrant, the bright pinks and blues of her clothing set like jewels on the society scene, her golden cape. Here, amid the brown paneling, the beige curtains, she feels rebuked, as if whoever set this up also inserted a cruel joke, turned her into a ridiculous parrot. A single piece of art hangs on the wall—a nude so luminously painted, the desire in the brushstrokes so palpable, that it is almost pornographic. The nude's face is partly obscured and turned to the window. Ashamed, Margot decides. Beneath the painting, instead of a couch, sit two of the ugliest chairs imaginable, upholstered in cheap dark red velvet, the kind they used in the old theaters back home. They unnerved her.

"Someone died in this apartment," she told her husband the first night, after she had tried to wash up in the too-small sink. "I can feel it."

"I don't want to hear anymore about the cursed mouse," her husband said.

"It's not about the mouse," she said. "A person died here."

"Don't be ridiculous, Margot."

"There are bloodstains on the porcelain."

"Where?"

She showed him.

Martin scratched the marks with his fingernail.

"Not blood, paint. This used to be an artists' studio."

"How do you know that?"

"I know the building owners."

"Who are they?"

Of course, he ignored her.

—————

Because she is still young and beautiful, the first thing she does is fill the apartment with mirrors: A full-length one by the door. Two in the hallway leading to the bedrooms. Even one in the kitchen.

"It will be good to see a familiar face now and then," she tells her husband.

"Too many eyes," her husband says. "You'll scare yourself again."

So when she wakes one night with the feeling of being watched, she decides to keep it to herself. But it happens again the following night. Not the mirrors. Something else. She sits up in bed, expecting to find Martin looking at her. But he is asleep, on his back, arms folded across his stomach, sleeping so soundly that for a moment, until she registers the rise and fall of his chest, she worries he is dead.

It's still dark out, but she rises to make the coffee. She works quietly in the kitchen, unsettled by the feeling that she is not alone. She turns slowly, letting her gaze pan past the small dining area. Something has changed, something has been moved in the sitting room. Something different about the ugly chairs. One of them is off-center, just a little bit, but enough for her to notice. When she moves it back into place, she sees that its cushion holds a slight imprint. Margot's heart beats in her throat. But she tries to calm down. Maybe she missed the detail last night when she was arranging the chairs. She fluffs the seat, moves it back into place, and tries to forget it. She won't mention it to Martin. He's been in a foul mood since they arrived in Miami Beach. He is doing some work for some organization, some training. He leaves early every morning and returns late, but never talks to her about any of it.

A few mornings later, the chair has moved again. And there is no mistake anymore: the imprint in the seat cushion is fresh and deep. She wants to call her mother, but this is forbidden. Meanwhile, Martin has started returning later and later in the evenings. Margot thinks perhaps he is already having an affair. This is the way her class is trained to think about things. She doesn't have the vocabulary for all the other possibilities. Someone is trying to torture her. Someone from the ERP . . . *This is crazy, Margot.* But the feeling of being watched doesn't leave her.

═══

"Could there be listening devices in the walls?" she asks Martin one evening after dinner.

"No," he says.

"I always feel eyes on me when I'm alone in the house; I feel thousands of eyes on me."

"As I said."

"It's not the mirrors. Something else."

"There's no such thing as ghosts, Margot."

"Not ghosts, but maybe cameras."

Martin doesn't say anything, but later that night he has a brief, whispered conversation with someone on the phone. The next morning he says, "Come, I'll drop you off at the library on my way in to work. It will do you good to get out of the apartment for a little bit. And there's no problem. We've even arranged for a library card."

We've.

And in fact, at the main desk, there is a card with her new name, and a welcome. Margot spends that morning in the history section. She attended a British school in B. and for a long time she was able to write more fluently in English than in Spanish. She wanted to be a writer, like the now-famous national one, but she found it too difficult to make words appear effortless and gave up. Anyway, the troubles had started by then, and her parents wanted her home. And then she married the sergeant ten years her senior and he wanted her home as well, because the troubles, and she blamed the troubles for the fact that they were unable to have children, though they tried, how they had tried when Martin was still full of joy!

≡

The visits to the library become regular and Margot's outlook improves. But every few mornings she wakes to find the imprint on the chair, the feeling of two invisible eyes hovering just above the seat, looking at her, *regarding* her, and she is chilled once again from the top of her head to the tips of her manicured fingers. One morning at the library, she decides to ask for help on some graduate research she's doing on the history of Miami Beach.

"What years are you looking at?" the old woman asks kindly.

Margot isn't sure when the Helena was built.

"I'm concentrating on the general development history of Miami Beach, so . . ."

The woman looks through one drawer and then another.

"I'd start with these from *The Miami Metropolis*, she says, handing Margot a box. Margot stares at it.

"You're a graduate student, you said?"

Margot nods.

"But this is your first time working with microfiche, am I right?"

Margot nods.

The woman looks her up and down.

"Come," she says.

It's not complicated. Margot gets the hang of it. And every morning she picks up a new round of film and goes through it, at first looking for any mention of the Helena, and then simply becoming absorbed in the story of the city. In this way, she learns that Collins was an actual person, John Collins, who planted an avocado grove. She reads about the first bridge from the mainland and how a man named Carl Fisher transported a special mechanical plow to pull up the mangroves. Over the weeks, Margot watches Miami Beach rise from the swamp in a blur of microfilm. Not so long ago, she realizes, the land where the Helena sits was full of wild rabbits and crocodiles sunning themselves on the shore. Developers in those early years staged outrageous stunts to attract buyers—one of them hired an elephant! As she scrolls fast past the years, she has the feeling of a fever, hers and Miami Beach's. The hubris of all that dredging and rerouting of the water: pumping boats, barges, oil tugs. And the fever doesn't let up as the weeks pass and the microfilm zips through the teens and the twenties, a city of white people and blue skys, and then the flappers in their frilly hats giving way to photographs of devastation—some terrible storm— and then back again to leisure: parties, grand buildings, and montages of white children playing in the sand, looked over by their nannies—the only Blacks in the photos. In time, Margot notices the ads. Here: an ad for the Green Heron, four hundred feet of private beach. "Garage—Daily Maid Service—Excellent Food" and at the bottom, a word Margot doesn't understand "—Gentiles—". The word appears again in a photograph of children playing on Española Way. In the background, a building looms, a sign painted on its façade: FURNISHED APARTMENTS MONTHLY RATES And beneath it: GENTILES ONLY.

And then one day, just like that, in the November 2, 1942, edition of the *Miami Herald*, a small story tucked between an ad for the Hotel Charles and the Stanton:

MYSTERIOUS DEATH OF MAJOR

The body of a Major in the US Army Air Corps was discovered at the Helena apartments near Flamingo Park in Miami Beach. John "Jack" Appleton, 32, was found in the kitchen of the Army-requisitioned apartment he shared with his bride, according to military police, who have taken the case. Sophie Appleton, 23, was taken in for questioning. The Army has not released additional details.

Margot's hands shake when she tries to advance the reel. She settles them in her lap and breathes until she feels well enough to shut off the machine.

That evening, she stands in the tiny, inadequate kitchen.

She covers the mirror there with a dishrag. But the feeling doesn't leave her. She throws open the cupboards, which are bare except for a cast-iron skillet. How long had it been there?

"I want you to get rid of this pan," she says to Martin, who is sitting at the pine table waiting for his dinner. "It's too heavy. I can't lift it."

"That's nonsense," he says. He enters the kitchen and lifts the pan. Margot flinches.

"What is wrong with you?" he says.

"Not with me," she says, "with the apartment. I think someone was murdered here."

"For god's sake, Margot, stop it."

Margot paces the kitchen. She stops suddenly, looking down.

"This is it," she screams.

"Keep your voice down, Margot."

Margot rubs the depression in the floor with her foot and then springs back.

"This is where the body must have fallen!" she says.

"You're not making any sense."

Martin stares at her for a long time.

"In the morning, all these mirrors are coming down," he says. "Now let's eat and stop discussing nonsense."

That evening, she covers the rest of the mirrors. But at night, Margot wakes alone and gasping for breath. Her dreams are haunted by all the things she refuses to see. Martin is not in their bed. Outside, the city shouts, but their bed remains still and cold. She rises carefully, trying to keep the floor from creaking beneath her. She walks slowly in her bare feet. Shadows everywhere. She stops in front of the red armchair. A figure there, outlined against the light. She takes an involuntary step back. But in the next moment she understands.

———

They will move again the following month, leaving 2B empty once more. Martin will take her to another Caribbean island and then to Paris, where they will live another fifteen years in a small set of rooms not far from the Luxembourg Gardens, the gardens where Martin will be shot by an unknown assassin—or perhaps just an ordinary thief—in 2004, the year ESMA becomes a human rights museum. His death, too, will emerge from the secret chambers of fate. She'll bury him and his false name in a small village outside Paris.

All those years she will lock up the memory of that night in Miami Beach, when, expecting to see a ghost, she found instead the figure of her husband.

He sits there even now: forever resting in the red velvet chair, half facing the window. The street's glow catches him in a faint spotlight. He sits straight, like a soldier, this husband she didn't know and never would. Margot watches him for a long time, waiting for him to turn and find her there. But he doesn't move. His eyes are open but fixed on something beyond. Some darkness that rests at the end of his field of vision. Darkness at the edge of everything he gazes upon. Margot crosses herself, again and again, and each night, she returns to bed alone.

SUSAN, 1988

That night, Susan Clark let her mind go slack, drift back in time, away from the knowledge that waited at the bottom of the stairs, looking up at her . . . She let her body remember him, rested in that memory, and, after, she enjoyed one of her deepest sleeps in years. Later, she woke in the dark. She'd been sweating and now was chilled in the artificially cooled room. The air-conditioning fan stopped suddenly. What a soothing monotony machinery provides. What terror when the silence returns. She threw aside the covers. Susan thought a noise had woken her. But it was the absence of sound. In the bathroom, she splashed her face with cold water. Back to the room, where she put on one of Tom's shirts. Never turning on the lights. She was so afraid of the dark as a child . . . Now she ran from the glare. Light sharp as a new blade. Tom's scent on her body. And below the bedroom window of apartment 2B, the sound of a car idling by the curb. Someone waiting. Something waiting.

Her daughter, Emily, is obsessed with Amelia Earhart.

"What I wanted to know is how does something that big *disappear*? How is it that you can lose a whole plane? For so many years? And what about all the memories that she took up into the sky with her? Where did they go?"

Susan sighs. "I'm not sure, honey. Some things are just unknowable."

"One of the books said that the plane could have landed somewhere secret. That would be better, don't you think? Some secret place. Because it would mean the plane was not lost, just hiding. Lost things can be found, even many years later. So maybe the plane is just lost. It's wrong to say it 'disappeared' unless no one really ever sees it again. Then it is a mystery what happened, then no one will know . . . Still, I don't think that's possible. Is it possible that something can vanish forever?"

"Yes," Susan says. "Some things can."

=====

When her daughter was five years old, Susan took her to a park by her parents' home. Tom had just left for . . . she wasn't supposed to know precisely, but of course she did. He moved them to Miami Beach to be closer to base. The U.S. started to send people like Tom over there, that much she gathered. We couldn't turn over Latin America to the Reds just like that, could we? But Miami was awful. The heat was awful. The mosquitoes were awful. So, without his permission or knowledge—he'd been gone for three months at that point and she'd had enough—Susan flew back to New Jersey, where her parents had retired by the shore. There was the park by their house. And Susan wanted fresh air. She was distracted. She doesn't recall the details now—just the blazing moment when Emily called to her. "Hello, Mommy, hello, Mommy!" Was it springtime? It must have been. The smell of some flowering thing in the air. The world going on with its renewal, indifferent to us. What a con, springtime. What stupid ecstasies people go into about it, all the while forgetting that the world mocks us, mocks our finality, our headlong rush—through ambition and envy and disappointment, and, yes, fleeting joys—straight to death.

"Hello, Mommy!" Susan reading, or talking to her mother. Probably her mother was with them. It doesn't matter. She followed the sound of Emily's voice, up, up to a ledge, more than a story up. A kind of ramp for a footbridge. And Emily was on the outside, on the other side of the railing, on the wrong side . . . Susan had known fear. But never the bottomless terror of a child happily calling your name one footfall from her death.

Not even now, with that soldier coming up the stairwell with a briefcase full of platitudes, the sound of his footfalls getting closer and closer. The soldier who will talk about her dead husband the way graduate students talk about dead artists. Not even that . . . A dead husband is a different terror. In the heart, in the mind, the soul, if you believe in that kind of luxury item. Terror on behalf of a child resides in the bowels, it comes from the genitals. The house of a child's birth remains ever attentive to her life. It makes no sense. What religion says that God resides in the bowels? There must be at least one . . .

Susan looked up at her daughter, at the edge of black, and felt something drop in the center of herself. But she remained calm. She wasn't in control now. What was in control? Susan Clark, unfortunately, did not believe in God, not even a God of the bowels. There is nothing, nothing after death. Nothing. But in life, in life, she believed, there was something that protected itself. What it is, we cannot know. But it guided Susan that day. "Emily, darling, don't move. Mommy will come get you." She didn't want to frighten the child. She didn't want to make her run away. One move, and she . . .

This was more than four years ago, and Susan still . . . She still wakes sometimes, just having fallen to sleep, with that image of Emily perched up there, so thin and helpless, driven on by curiosity, exposed like a little flightless bird. And Susan always startles herself awake and then cannot sleep for hours, sometimes the entire night, thinking, And what if she had not called to me? And what if I had yelled out and startled her? And in that imagined terror, in that image of Emily falling, Susan finds gratitude. The only authentic gratitude she has ever known. Because that day, she rescued her daughter. Even if death was already stalking them . . . that day it didn't ensnare them.

After a tragedy people always say, If only he left the house two minutes earlier. If only the convoy was not delayed by paperwork . . . That's how people are. Time has joints. But we only see them in misfortune. Well, Susan saw it that day when they cheated death. She saw something about time. It's reticulated, like that skeleton of the tiger python she saw as a child in a London museum. It bends at certain places. And sometimes you do leave the house two minutes earlier. You just don't know it. You don't know enough to be grateful, so you just arrive at your destination, complaining about the traffic like a stupid ox.

Emily. How will Susan tell her? Emily and her father felt a bond that Susan couldn't match or even understand. They had been working on a book of missing places, lost homelands . . . It's as if he knew . . . as if he were preparing the text for her. Emily reads it every night and Susan sits by her bed and listens to the things her husband meant to say . . . Missing in action. Presumed dead. What do these words mean? Words are a shroud. We throw them over the thing itself, sometimes to give it shape, more often to obscure it. Does she believe in omens? Is that the form religion takes in the unreligious? Yes. Susan did not believe in gods, but she believed in omens. Something in the patterns of the world, something she felt too stupid to know.

Susan Clark grew up on the Upper East Side in a three-bedroom ensconced in the family for two generations. Loaded, what they call it now. Just rich when she was a girl. Sometimes with the word *filthy* attached to it. So now *loaded* sounds like a step up to Susan. It's all words . . . shrouds . . . casting shadows . . . Her mother was attentive . . . but she cared for her with a distracted kind of love. She was probably an alcoholic—so many women became alcoholics in the 1950s, that perfect decade. And she maintained rigid ideas about the proper way a girl's room should look: neat, clean. Toys more as decoration than comfort. Appearances . . . Susan's toys were of the finest quality. Too fine for play.

For her seventh birthday, her aunt and uncle gifted Susan a doll. Until then, most dolls that came into her life were hard, decorative objects. But this one had the charm of being made of rubber. Susan held her . . . Practice? Is that all life is? A practice? To what end? But Susan held her . . . held her, and the gentle yield of the doll against her chest gave her a feeling she never forgot. A thing to hold. Not as bulwark against loneliness or suffering. Thank god she didn't know those big-ticket words as a child—the words that came to ruin her. Just to hold.

The following week, they set off, as usual, to summer in the Riviera. She wanted to bring her doll to Europe—she named her Melissa—but her mother said no. The doll was ordered back in her packaging and placed on a top shelf in Susan's closet.

When the family returned in August, Susan raced to hold her doll. Melissa was still there, in her wooden box. But when Susan took her out, she saw that the New York City summer had altered her irrevocably. Not yielding, not soft. Time carves skulls out of our playthings. Susan, the little girl, could scarcely look at this shrunken brittle thing. Stiff from waiting, she thought. From hopelessness. Only the doll's blue glass eyes remained unchanged . . . and when, in a fit, Susan threw her to the floor, the eyes in that shattered face suddenly opened, gazing up at her, astonished . . .

═══

The apartment has the exact layout as all the other apartments in the Helena. Though they're renting, she's made some changes. The large closet in the main bedroom she's turned into an office. And by the front door, Susan has set two open bookcases to break the view into the rest of the space, a clever decorating trick that creates an intimate and private welcome.

On one of the shelves, silver frames hold photos of a young, bearded man. In one, he stands in a jungle, an enormous backpack looming over his head. Into this sanctuary, now, that other soldier enters.

═══

It's Saturday. Emily will have the weekend to understand and mourn. And when the school year is over, Susan will break the lease on this apartment and move back to her parents' place in New Jersey.

"Come here, baby," Susan says. "Mommy needs to tell you something. It's about Daddy."

"He's coming back for me next week." Emily says, her mouth set. "His missions are so secret that he can't even tell us, but I know."

Susan sits down on Emily's bed. Her room resembles a tasteful, minimalist bachelor pad: all polished bamboo and black accents, a white comforter on a simple daybed. Nothing frilly or pink. A bookcase covers an entire wall. The only concession to her age and time is a Duran Duran poster on the wall.

But today Emily doesn't want to talk about her missing father. She wants to talk about the Electra. Susan tries to avoid thinking of air disasters, even ones that happened decades ago. But she, too, wants to put off the truth.

"They left from right here. Isn't that awesome?" Emily says. "Miami to San Juan to Caripito—that's in Venezuela—and then on and on: Fortaleza and Natal before flying to Saint-Louis in Senegal. Then across the African continent: Dakar, Khartoum, and then Assab to Karachi. The first nonstop flight over the Red Sea!"

"I didn't know any of this," Susan says.

"It's in the books," Emily says. "Calcutta, Bangkok, Singapore. And on through some different places in the Dutch East Indies—I forget—until the leg from Darwin to Lae."

Emily's been counting off the cities on her fingers and stops to look at her mother.

"So, they took off from Lae on July 2, 1937, at ten a.m. local time. That's midnight GMT. So eight p.m. in Miami. The clock goes backwards when you move west. Lae, New Guinea, is fourteen hours ahead of Miami, so all you have to do is change a.m. to p.m. and subtract or add two."

Emily takes a breath. Her voice becomes more high-pitched

and she's talking faster, as if racing to tell a story that she's already been told to cut short.

"I've been calculating time zones in my head. It relaxes me," she says. It doesn't take special brains, just a system."

Susan smiles. "I agree. You don't need brains if you have a system." She pats Emily's hand, though the girl has already complained that this makes her feel like a baby and she's not a baby anymore. But today, Emily doesn't complain. She's being gentle with her mom. Susan holds Emily's hand, which seems unusually warm tonight, but Susan won't register that until later.

"Precisely," says Emily. The word all wrong for a ten-year-old, but the word that precisely describes her. "For most of Europe (excepting England), it's simple: I just picture a clock and move it ahead to the number directly opposite. So three p.m. in Miami is nine p.m. in Paris. That's easy. Once you've mastered this system, then other time zones are a piece of cake. It helps to know your geography: Kuala Lumpur, Beijing, Lhasa, Singapore, and Perth all share a time zone with Hong Kong: They are all exactly a half day ahead of Miami. Paris, Amsterdam, Berlin, all six hours. Iraq is just one hour ahead of Europe: Baghdad, Kuwait City, Riyadh, all of those are seven hours ahead of Miami. So, you put yourself in Paris and add an hour . . . Like everything, it gets easier the more you practice."

Emily stops and looks up at her mother.

Susan takes her in her arms. "Oh, honey. We need to talk about—"

But Emily stands suddenly. "Wait, Mommy! I want to show you something."

Mommy. She hasn't called her that in years.

Emily takes a book down from the shelf and sits next to Susan.

The book is bound and covered by a brocade fabric upon which is stitched, in curly letters, the title, *An Atlas of Imaginary Lands.* Tom made all of it by hand.

Emily opens the book. "I'm going to read to you about Flozella," she says. "You should know that Flozella is an island on earth, but since it is imaginary, it is not an island on the earth we know, but on one of many, many possible earths . . . Everything that can happen does. Every possibility in time exists. Do you believe that, Mommy?"

"I'm not sure," Susan says.

"Okay. I'll give you an example. Take the plane. In one of those countless earths, the Electra took off from Lae at ten a.m. July second, 1937, Amelia and Fred had an emergency on board and simply headed for the island of Flozella, where they managed to land the plane without a hitch . . . On another earth, the plane turned north and is sitting on a runway in Vietnam. On another earth, the plane turned around and landed safely again in Lae. On another earth, Amelia managed to land the plane on the water, and she and her navigator were rescued by fishing boats that trailed bright red banners. On another earth, nothing at all happened; the flight was like any other. After taking off, it cruised normally and arrived at Howland Island two thousand miles later and Amelia got off and went on with her life, all her big and small worries, all her memories. Maybe she and Fred fought about the almost-accident they had, all the time not knowing that their time twins had gotten to the end of their stories."

Emily takes a deep breath but doesn't clear her throat. She begins reading in a strong, assured voice.

"Flozella is part of an island chain in the South Pacific, first discovered by Herman Melville. Today, the bloodthirsty Mardians rule there, a stern, joyless people who have terrorized the population by banning all happy things. But in the times before history, other creatures populated that distant island chain, beings with enormous wings spanning the height of a coconut palm."

Emily looks up at her mother and smiles.

"Some people think the winged beings did not perish completely. There's a small island chain off Flozella, an archipelago so small that it does not appear on maps. For half the day, the islands lie submerged beneath the waters and the winged creatures rest on the wind. But in twilight, the islands emerge from the sea, their streets and homes washed clean. And then the creatures can finally alight on their enchanted land, where for the next twelve hours, they will rest and dine and be kind to one another . . ."

Emily closes the book.

"Do you know what this other island chain is called? Allez Olf . . . funny isn't it? Sounds like French, right? But here, look, if you read it, you see it's just Flozella spelled backwards . . . This other island chain lies six nautical miles west of Flozella, in the middle of the Pacific. On the map it just looks like end-less sea . . . but here is where all the missing things go . . . This is the next entry we are going to write, Dad and I."

Emily stands and slides the book back on the shelf. But Susan's eyes go to a box sitting near it. It's painted in shades of blue and red and reminds her of something.

"Who gave you that box?" Susan says. "I don't think I've ever seen it before."

Emily seems to hesitate.

"Dad," she says.

"Dad?" Susan says.

"A little while ago," Emily says.

"Before he left?" Susan tries to stand but cannot. "What do you mean, Dad?"

"Dad visited me a few nights ago and taught me how to decorate it."

"Oh, honey, you were dreaming."

Emily shakes her head. "Was not. He was in uniform. Said not to say anything to you. He was between assign-ments . . . I'm not supposed to say, but it's a magic box."

Susan's body has gone cold and the room is unstable. Not spinning, exactly, but watery. She's watching her daughter through the porthole of a submarine descending.

Emily sees her mother grow pale. "Are you okay?"

"No," Susan says. "I'm not. There's something . . ."

Emily stands. "Please don't be upset, Mommy."

She takes the box down from the shelf and hands it to her mother.

"Daddy didn't want to scare you."

Susan accepts the box in her cold hands. It is much heavier than it looks, as if it were filled with glass.

When she tries to shake it, Emily takes it back gently.

"Inside are some things we've lost," she says.

"Things we've lost?"

"Precisely," Emily says. "We lost them in this world, and they ended up in here."

Emily taps the box lightly.

"The pair of earrings that you lost on vacation, remember?

Susan doesn't say anything.

"They're in here now," Emily says. "So is the toy bunny I left at Burdines. Other things, too, they're all in here . . ."

Emily's pale, long fingers hold the box as if it were a moonbeam.

"The thing is, even though we know what's in it, we must never open the box."

Emily looks at her mother, who stares back at her.

"The moment you open the box," Emily says in a patient voice, "the lost things disappear forever."

After a moment Emily stands and returns the box to the shelf. She turns to Susan.

"Are you crying, Mommy?"

Susan blinks a few times. She senses, with terrible urgency, that more losses lie ahead. In the slanting afternoon light Emily's eyes, watching her, are a startling, watery blue.

Apartment 2B settles into itself. The light inside dims—a passing cloud shadow. These rooms are rarely empty. Painters, models, artists, mothers, fathers, strangers. For decades now, always someone wearing down the pine floors, someone's breath disturbing the air. No one thinks that homes also need pauses, pockets of silence. Homes also need time to gather themselves, time to simply rest. All that sheltering and holding, that gets exhausting.

MARILYN, 1994

Marilyn Aranjuez and Derek Williams leave the Helena, and, as they walk along Flamingo Park, have a small argument over where to go for dinner. It's almost midnight—both are junior lawyers and they've been working late again. Derek is tired and just wants to grab a quick bite at the News Café, but Marilyn wants to check out the newly renovated Delano.

"Anne told me it's very sexy—white curtains everywhere, the most beautiful people," Marilyn says to Derek, who walks with his hands in his pockets. "Madonna was at the opening party!"

Marilyn is twenty-five and her real life has finally started to match the one in her head. Last year, she left her family home in Kendall and moved with Derek into apartment 2B, a decision that so scandalized her conservative family they stopped speaking to her for two months. Her mother relented a bit when she met Derek: "He looks like Cary Grant!" And she began to take her daughter's calls again, but she hadn't told anyone in the family about her daughter's living arrangements.

Marilyn loved this part of the story—loved the aura of danger it gave her—as far back as family history went, no woman had ever lived outside her father's home before marriage.

It is a spring night, and the temperature is still pleasant, the streets lit up by soft streetlights and a full moon.

"Look at that," she says, pointing at a balcony where geraniums are exploding.

"The Delano is needlessly expensive," Derek says, not looking up. "It's late. We won't even enjoy it."

That's the thing with Derek. He may be handsome, but he's impossibly cheap. Take this Deco dump he lives in, when there are so many better options on Brickell that would also put them closer to work. Lately he's been working through the weekends—billing hours to pay down his law school debts more quickly. But all the work leaves him tired, too tired for sex, which Marilyn, who was chaperoned until she turned twenty-one, really enjoys. "Fine," Marilyn says. "Fine, fine, fine. We'll eat some greasy junk at the News Café, and it will be fine."

From a back alley comes the insistent screech of a car alarm, the four-part disharmony that's been fouling every evening. It cycles to the end, *beep beep beep*, and then starts again until someone shuts it off.

Derek looks in the direction of the sound but doesn't say anything more. And Marilyn is consoled by her secret: tomorrow, after Derek flies to the Caymans to take a deposition, she and G. will drive to the Keys. She didn't intend any of it; it was as if the fates planned it while she was barely conscious. The heart is ungovernable and will is an illusion.

That's how Marilyn sees it. Look at old, wrinkled Margaret and handsome Mr. Daney at the firm! There are enough unlikely pairings and startling, sudden desires in this life to make you believe that mischievous gods still move about our world, unburdening their poisoned darts.

Marilyn and G. had been working together on a complicated zoning case since December, and she was moved by his gentle manner. So many of the lawyers she knew were like short, fat fuses, always sparking this way and that. Not G., who gave off a slow heat. He looked at her when she spoke, and he waited until she was done to speak himself. He was smart. She was smart. They were young, all of them at the firm, and lovely. G. was lovely—work was before them, but Marilyn was unable to look away from his full lips. They lunched downtown with the clients. Drove there in his Miata. Another lunch with the same clients. Then lunch just the two of them, at a Peruvian place, to discuss strategy. And then drinks on Brickell one night while Derek was traveling. And another time, a Saturday when Derek was working late—again—drinks at the new Van Dyke's, where they sat upstairs to listen to the jazz, a cover of Billie Holiday, all whiskey-melt and glamorous suffering. And after, they went for a walk on Lincoln Road, and G. put his arm around her waist, at first to help her over a puddle, and when she turned to face him, he held her gaze for a moment and then pulled her close.

"Watch out!" Derek shouts, and pulls her back on the sidewalk.

The car nearly sideswipes them.

"Fucker!" Derek shouts after them.

At the News Café, they take the last table outside. At the next table sit two young men, hands entwined. Marilyn watches them. The one in the cut-off T-shirt is almost painfully handsome. He seems to know it, too, and as he bends in for another kiss, his eye catches Marilyn's. What joy in his face!

Derek orders his usual, a fried egg sandwich, and Marilyn orders a tomato soup.

"I'm not very hungry," she says, still sulking because it makes her feel less guilty. If only to be as happy and free as those handsome lovers!

"If not the Delano, we could have at least gone to Van Dyke's."

"Food is the same as here, owners the same," Derek says.

"It's not as dingy."

Derek shrugs. "Next time, then."

"They play jazz upstairs."

"Oh?" But he doesn't ask Marilyn how she knows this. Instead, he looks at her for a moment.

"Why are you being like this?" He says it so softly that she can pretend not to hear.

It's almost two in the morning when they trudge back up Eighth and then along the park under the canopy of Brazilian beautyleaf—of course Derek would know the name of these gnarled trees. Marilyn walks with her hands behind her back. They've almost reached the Helena when they hear the car. Engine revving as it gets closer, and then the squeal of tires. Derek turns first, ready to unleash his frustration—what is wrong with Marilyn tonight?—on these inconsiderate strangers.

It's a van, not a car. It stops in front of them. Later, Marilyn and Derek will not be able to agree on the color. Or on how many jump out of it. They will remember only that they were young men, boys really. That they all carried white PVC piping except for the one who pointed the gun.

A pistol. Marilyn sees the glint off it and her body dissolves into warm piss.

"Oh my god, please."

Derek steps in front of her, protecting. He doesn't say anything. No one says anything, that's how Marilyn will remember it for years. No one talks or shouts. The boys surround Derek and beat him with the plastic pipes. When he turns his back to them, they strike him across the kidneys.

"Oh god, please, no," Marilyn says.

The sky and street are rotating. Time condenses. From out of the past, an old safety lesson, born in her 1970s childhood, in the aftermath of serial killers and the unheeded cries of Kitty Genovese. The police officer telling the six-year-olds to never scream for help because cries for help only scare people away. *When in danger, scream,* Fire! Help *makes people lock their doors.* Fire *brings out the curious.*

The boys are beating Derek. Everyone silent. A ballet of the mute. In the buildings gathered around them, all the windows are dark.

"Fire," Marilyn screams. "Fire, fire, fire." Her throat burning.

Like a spell broken, the boys stop. The van door slides open. The boys run inside. A maroon van, or a blue one, silver perhaps. And Marilyn and Derek run to their building, where all the shades are down and no one comes to help them, not even the curious. Keys shaking in her hands, she tries the door. The keys fall to the grass. The van starts again. Derek finds the keys, opens the door. They don't remember going up the stairs. They don't remember opening the door to their apartment. She calls the police from the phone in the kitchen, though Derek says not to bother, he's okay. They are asleep on the couch when the police ring downstairs at six thirty in the morning, sun coming up over South Beach.

By then Derek's skin is abloom in purples and blues. The police take photos—nothing will come of them.

When Marilyn asks the cops what took them so long, one of them says, "Give us a break, lady, we had two homicides tonight."

When they leave, Derek sits on the couch, his eyes unfocused. He says his head hurts and Marilyn tells him to lie down. He nods but doesn't move. He seems far away, cloaked in loneliness. When he lifts his eyes, Marilyn sees the baffled fear, and she understands in an instant that it is not the boys' doing, but her own.

In a few hours, Derek will leave for the Caymans—his father was an officer in Normandy, and he didn't raise a hysteric. After, alone in the apartment, Marilyn will call G. and cancel the trip to the Keys. But now she rubs ice on Derek's bruises. Gently, back and forth, water pooling over his hot skin.

Homes also dream; they shelter themselves. Apartment 2B sleeps and wakes in a castle. The floor is hard but smooth, smoother than the most perfect ice, though this slippery veil is warm, like a sun. Its walls are made of the same material, a hard, smooth surface that refracts light from a hidden source. The translucence is cut here and there by shards of red and blue light, slivers of orange and yellow, a thousand rainbows endlessly repeated in the crevices. The walls are smooth and unmarred by windows, the room is suffused by the mysterious light, which works like a shiver down to the foundations of apartment 2B. A doorway without a door leads to a long corridor of perfect proportions. And behind that room, another room, equal to the first, where the light is stronger, pulsing like a heartbeat. And behind that another corridor and more rooms, endless rooms, each identical to the first, each made of this hard-polished glass that grows more and more alive, the light refracting and re-forming. Apartment 2B is a castle of sublime limpidity, and the rooms connect one to another like diamonds on a string, infinite.

BEATRICE, 2002

Her name is not on the lease. In the strict language of real estate law, Beatrice Dumonts is an unauthorized tenant. The official tenants of apartment 2B are Maribel Rodriguez and Ignacio Salas: a recently married couple in their thirties (well, early forties in the case of Maribel, though as sycophants are quick to insist, she could easily pass for a decade younger). Beatrice, twenty-four years old, is Ignacio's girlfriend.

Confusing, it's true. But not any more confusing than immigration law, which granted citizenship to Maribel for the accident of her Cuban birth and has so far denied it to Ignacio (Colombia) and Beatrice (Haiti).

So for a flat fee of $5,000 (plus the cost of the ceremony, which came to another $2,000) Maribel agreed to marry Ignacio and to remain married for the time required by law, after which they would meet with an immigration officer who, with a few impertinent questions, would verify that the couple were legitimately married and grant Ignacio a green card. Then they will proceed with the divorce.

For the last two years, Maribel and Ignacio have slept in separate bedrooms of their common household. Two months ago, Beatrice joined them in apartment 2B after her landlord, citing new regulations instigated by the terrorist attacks, demanded proof of citizenship. Now, with the hearing less than a month away, the happy couple is in the process of establishing the facts of their marriage.

Ignacio has discussed the situation with a few trusted friends. The times are such that they cannot afford to make any mistakes. He has an idea, and he broaches it first with Maribel.

"The investigators are brutal," Ignacio begins. "It's not a matter of memorizing a few 'facts,' these guys are specially trained."

"We'll wing it, don't worry," Maribel says. They are sitting at the dining room table, Beatrice taking a nap in Ignacio's small bedroom.

"That's easy for you to say," Ignacio says. "If we fuck this up, they'll deport me. Hell, they might bring me up on terrorism charges, why not? These are not times for fucking around."

"You're catastrophizing."

"You're sticking your head in the sand."

Beatrice surprises them.

"Look at you two," she says, "fighting like the long-married couple you're not."

—————

The reception was held in the backyard of some friends of Maribel's—some grand house in Coral Gables. Cubans. High fence to keep away . . . who? What? Two-story house hidden behind bougainvilleas, gloriously in bloom. The backyard stretched almost the length of the city block. A tasteful oblong pool shaded by palm trees on one side and a gazebo on the other. A gazebo that might have easily sheltered two families anywhere else in the world.

Ignacio paid the guy, of course. He also arranged for a trio of Ecuadorians to make a party-sized paella by the pool. As a wedding gift, the owners decorated the yard and the gazebo, where a notary (a cousin of Maribel's) pronounced the crone and Beatrice's boyfriend man and wife. Beatrice attended as a guest, but not alone. She brought along a friend, a man she worked with at the restaurant who, Beatrice knew, was a little bit in love with her. Beatrice loved the small gasps they produced when they walked in. They looked good together and everyone knew it. Especially Maribel, who glanced at them, frowned, and then ignored them for the rest of the evening. Ignacio seemed not to notice, which Beatrice took for evidence of very good acting, the kind of acting animated by jealousy.

The whole party was supposed to last just an hour, enough to get the photos to prove this was no sham marriage. But it stretched late into night, as friends of the owners kept crashing for the booze and food. The party didn't end until the police showed up to address the neighbors' noise complaints. Maribel, who must have been drunk by then, raised a toast and said something about how this would be a great story to tell their grandkids. As if anyone believed that old coconut could still make babies.

"Look," Ignacio says, "we'll keep our street clothes under the PJs."

"You're totally nuts," Maribel says.

"We've sacrificed for more than two years," Ignacio says. "I don't want to throw it away now."

"I'm not trying to throw anything away," Maribel says. "I just don't think it's a good idea for us to sleep in the same bed."

"It would be just for a week or two," Ignacio says.

"You've told Beatrice about this?"

"Not until you agree . . . why upset her?"

Maribel laughs. "It's not necessary to sleep in the same bed, trust me. You're freaking out for no reason. It's a routine hearing, not the Inquisition. They ask you about what side of the bed you each sleep on, that sort of thing. I have friends who have been through this."

Ignacio is pacing up and down the tiny dining room. "Your friends went through this before the world blew up," he says. "Now these guys are on hyper-alert."

"You're going to wear out the floor."

"I'm nervous, okay?"

"Iggy, darling, husband dear," she says with a smile. "We just need to memorize a script: *Yes, sometimes Ignacio snores, but only when he sleeps on his back. And, yes, I sleep on the right side of the bed and always wake up an hour before Maribel to prepare her breakfast. What does she eat? She prefers yogurt and granola, though on weekends, I'll go down to Sixth Street to buy us pastelitos.*"

"Three nights," Ignacio says. "Please. It would calm me down." And then, as an afterthought, he adds, "I would be the perfect gentleman, if that's what you're worried about. Just two nights. One night, even."

―――

Maribel is alone in the apartment. She has already finished two cups of oolong tea and started on a third. She holds the cup with both hands, enduring the burn, knowing it won't last.

She started the yoga fifteen years ago. A lot of women do it to stay slim. Others come to yoga at the end of a spiritual quest, tired of listening to the intellect, hungry for the body's story. Maribel came to yoga hoping to find a way out of the desire that tormented her, that persisted through disappointment and experience, that tugged at her when she was most vulnerable to its honeyed advances.

No, it would not be a good idea to share a bed with Ignacio.

―――

The lock tumbles. Ignacio steps inside, his first footsteps sending a shivering groan through the floor, though he doesn't notice. What he does notice is the unusual quiet that follows it. A deep, resting quiet that to Ignacio feels alive. As if there were something else already there, something waiting to wake. He senses this without being able to put thoughts on it. A feeling that is both terrifying and exciting. He walks quickly across the living room and into the kitchen, where he flips on the light to drive away the morning gloom. He makes himself a cup of coffee and sits at the table.

Ignacio can't remember the last time he was alone in the apartment. One of the women is always around, often both. Now that he's alone, he realizes he likes it. That feeling of warmth and joy he thought he felt in their company seems, in solitude, to more resemble anxious waiting. Always someone watching him, someone ready to be misunderstood, insulted, hurt. He didn't realize until this moment, how much he has come to measure his words these last two months. How little of his thoughts he shares. He cannot even be sure now of what he really thinks or feels—all of it seems caught up in public transactions. It is as if he were one of those performance artists, continuously onstage, acting the part of himself. And that audience behind the glass: they know so little about him. Even Ignacio knows only partial truths. And there are things he doesn't even tell himself, events he has worked so hard to erase that when their memory surfaces, he can easily imagine that he saw it in a movie, that they happened to someone else.

Maybe it is good that he is so rarely alone. Because now, in solitude, Ignacio begins to think, and when he begins to think, he begins to worry. And maybe this is the way his father went insane: alone, spinning stories in the dark. A flickering frontier separates reality from imagination. It's not only true in the Caribbean. Those who live in the borderlands know that all reality is magical, all madness an ordinary country.

His first love was Rebecca, in kindergarten. She was a red-haired fairy in a sea of brunettes. Exotic, though he didn't know the word then. Unattainable, though he would not be able to describe her that way. The words for it didn't yet exist for him, but the feeling did, and it was a feeling that Ignacio would return to again and again, involuntarily, over the course of his life. The pull to the different, the irrational longing, the pursuit, followed always by the disappointment. It's not that people are too different. It's that they're not different enough.

Ignacio stands and stretches. How long has he been lost to himself? It could be five minutes or five hours. Ignacio is afraid to look at the clock. One of the women will be home soon. He goes to the kitchen, makes himself a sandwich and a café con leche, and stands at the counter to eat. When he's finished, he washes his plate, dries it, and puts it away. Maribel has already noted this behavior. Perhaps later she will joke with the immigration officer about her husband's OCD and all of them will have a chummy laugh. What neither of the women understand is that his need for order is a response to the disorder in his thoughts. His incessant back-and-forth, his inability to concentrate on one thing for very long. His mind is always hopping from one thing to another. If he can discipline the world, maybe he will learn to discipline his mind.

He dries his hands and pulls a rag from beneath the sink. He's the only one who cleans around here. As soon as the thought forms, he laughs. In moments like this, caught between thoughts, he realizes how strange this whole setup is. Right now, standing with the cloth in his hands, Ignacio feels like the drunk man struck suddenly sober. Just what do they think they're doing, the three of them? What mad caper are they writing for themselves? How will it all end?

And if you looked at them from the outside you wouldn't know what to think. Could be recently arrived cousins sharing an apartment. They even talk the same Caribbean Spanish—Beatrice having lived five years in the D.R. before arriving in Miami. And yet Maribel is the one who gets the papers. What a ridiculous notion, nationality. Ignacio now sees the entire apparatus of nationhood—with its pitiful pride and traditions and sense of exceptionalism—as an absurd historical joke. He knows this brief flash of sobriety won't last, so he basks for a moment in its light. Where does nation end? What is it really made of? What if nations were organized by accents? All those who understand the phrase 'sta 'qui 'atra stand over here. You are now a nation. Or by favorite childhood memories? Nations of fourth-grade swimmers in this corner. Or by professions? Ignacio has much more in common with engineers, no matter what supposed nation they're from, than he has with artists from his own country.

And then just like that Ignacio's simple clarity vanishes. Who would organize such nations? How would you tax them? What a horrific place to live: the Nation of Engineers. Sta Qui Atra wouldn't mean anything special in a nation where that was just the way people talked. Stupid Saturday morning thoughts.

Ignacio is better when he's working, not thinking. He moves to the dining room, swipes the rag across the table, then the tops of the chairs, the tops of the frames that sit on the table by the sofa. Photos of his parents and Maribel's parents, as any married couple would display, making sure to keep the balance. Not too much from his side. Not too much from hers. And is it appropriate to turn down the face of his mother-in-law when his wife is not home?

And the photo of his father. Taken in Cartagena a year before his illness. Ignacio picks it up, searching the face. After a long moment, he dusts the frame, slowly, impassively, as if it held a stranger's image. He returns it to the tabletop without making a sound.

Ignacio has never told anyone about his father. Not even Beatrice. Especially not Maribel. His father was a brilliant painter—everyone said so, though by the time Ignacio was born he rarely made it to the studio, spending hours on the chaise lounge in his study, staring at the ceiling. This taciturn, quiet figure was the only father Ignacio had ever known. But all these years later, the years of immobility and distance seem to have condensed to a single memory. So that when Ignacio thinks back on his childhood, the more vivid memories are of the days when his father was well. When Ignacio returned from school to find him cooking something wonderful in the kitchen. When his smile greeted him as if he were the loveliest child in the world. On those days, Ignacio would be filled with a new kind of energy. His father would sweep him onto the couch and read him adventure books. Or sit with him at the dining room table making dozens of tiny swans and bears out of colored paper. Those are the days that still vibrate in Ignacio's memory.

No one talked about it—not his grandmother and not Ignacio's mother. Much later, Ignacio learned of the electroshock treatments. The sadness that was a stone in the throat. That's why Ignacio keeps moving. When the darkness threatens to close him off, he stops thinking. Starts doing.

=====

Maribel's voice startles Ignacio out of the past.

"I canceled my afternoon class," she says. "Such a beautiful day, I didn't see the point of being inside a stinky studio, you know! Anyway, only three students showed up. Those sad middle-aged types that come to everything. I couldn't deal today. Thought I'd come by and if you were around, take you to lunch. So, what a nice surprise! You are home!"

She was Maribel, talking without pausing to hear answers to questions she never bothers to ask outright. Smiling like that. Same smile these last few days. Ignacio can't be sure if it's happiness or madness—so finely attuned as he is to the latter. But there's something new in her. Something charged, electric. Perhaps she's fallen in love. Maribel in love? Ignacio feels a ghostly whisper of—what? Jealousy? Where the hell did that come from? Thankfully, as soon as he applies his mind to it, it vanishes. Some atavistic holdover, some weird semantic baggage that comes automatically attached to the idea of "wife" even if this idea of wife is not his, not the present idea of wife. But is that so? Is the historical understanding of "wife" any different from the arrangement that he finds himself in now? Isn't the long history of marriage, in fact, one of conveniently executed contracts? This revelation makes Ignacio smile now. This possibility that he has, in fact, entered into the most traditional of marriages—one of convenience, a very old setup distinguished only by the fact that in this case, it was he who paid the dowry.

And now his thoughts have become as run-on and unformed as Maribel's talk. Is it possible that she could infect him like this with her personality, even though they are not really man and wife? Even though they have entered a marriage without love, without memories, a dry business agreement. A fraud, if one is to be precise (Ignacio cannot help being precise)—a fraud that will never be consummated.

"Hello? Anyone home?" Maribel snaps her fingers in front of Ignacio's eyes. "So how about it?"

"It?"

"Lunch, silly!" She smiles. When Maribel smiles, she looks fifteen years younger. Her smile is guileless, spontaneous.

"I feel I've been neglecting my poor husband."

She says this last in the same cheerful tone. But something about her expression at the word *husband* penetrates deep into Ignacio. Dislodges something in his chest. Several moments tick past. Lunch, sure, why not?

———

Beatrice returns from the breakfast shift to find the apartment empty. Strange. Ignacio has always been home at this hour. She scans the room. Everything neatly lined up on the shelves. Silver frames on the photos gleaming, like on a movie set. Ignacio's nerves again. Beatrice supposes she should be happy. Her girlfriends all complain that their men are slobs. She should count herself lucky. But something about the neatness unsettles her. It's not natural. It's not normal to seek after so much order, it goes against all the laws of reality, it is a rejection of the natural way of things. Everything arises and perishes, all striving turns to dust. Her own beauty, of which she is so proud, her own beauty is already fading. Imperceptibly to everyone, perhaps, but not to her.

Miami Beach. How did she end up here? Late one night at the restaurant, Betsy told Beatrice how her mother used to have to carry identification to be allowed to stay on the beach. *People like us—they turned us out like animals after dark. They still don't want us here.* Beatrice, always running, unwanted, from one place to the next.

It is only one in the afternoon, but she pours herself a drink, strong enough to strangle memory. Sometimes she worries that she will become an alcoholic. But even that would be better than having to live with the memories that have not lost their sting after all these years. No, no, the drink is good. The drink is better than the images. The drink quiets those voices that are always ready to pull her back into the past. A long dark road, muddy tracks. A lone figure ahead. And then another. And another. The fading light casting long shadows of their weapons as they move slowly toward her. Light falling, falling, and Beatrice falling with it, the figures only shadows. Figments. Vanishing like puffs of smoke.

Beatrice is asleep on the couch when Maribel and Ignacio

return from lunch, so she does not see Maribel's flush and cannot speculate on its cause.

═══

Beatrice is getting ready for work when Ignacio steps into the room.

"Are you leaving already? Isn't it early?" he asks.

She buttons her blouse.

"I agreed to work two shifts today. Some big group is celebrating a retirement or something," she says. "I'll be back around midnight."

Ignacio sits on the edge of the bed. It's a full-sized bed, too small for two adults, but this is where they've been sleeping every night since Beatrice moved in, though they never make love at night, not when Maribel is in the house.

"Come sit with me for a moment," he says. "I need to talk to you about something."

Beatrice checks her watch and joins him on the edge of the bed. Ignacio strokes her hand, not looking at her.

"I talked to Raúl. The immigration hearing is in two weeks," he says, still not looking at her. "Things are very, very hairy right now. There's a lot of scrutiny after the attacks, a lot of deportations, a lot of arrests."

"Okay," she says. "Well, that's why you have a lawyer, right? You want me to say everything's going to be fine, or what?"

Ignacio turns to Beatrice.

"Look, Bea, Raúl doesn't know about our setup—he's not

supposed to know anything about our setup, you understand? But he let me understand that the questions have gotten really, really tough. The agents are asking for really specific details about the marriage—not just, you know, about intimacy, but about everything, stuff you can't prepare for."

"Okay . . . so?"

"Raúl wanted to make sure that Maribel and I are sleeping in the same room. He specifically said that—"

Beatrice stands up.

"You want to spend the night with the old coconut, then."

"Please, Bea."

"*Please, Bea*," she says. "I've always liked when you beg."

"I'm really sorry about this," Ignacio says.

"Yes," Beatrice says. "So am I."

"Please, can you try to understand?"

Bea turns her back to him. In a moment she's at the mirror, putting on her makeup. Ignacio watches her shoulders rise and fall as she takes deep breaths.

She turns to him at last.

"My god," Ignacio says. "You look beautiful."

"Yes," she says. She watches Ignacio for a while. And then she bends down to kiss him on the forehead, marking him.

"Look, Iggy, I understand. I trust you to decide what's best. If Raúl says this is important, then do what you need to do."

"It's just for the weekend," he says. "We'll wear our street clothes under our pajamas."

"Okay, baby," she says.

He walks carefully across the bare pine floor, aware now of every creak. The door to Maribel's bedroom is half-open. Maribel's bedside lamp is on. She is lying very still, turned toward the wall away from the door. She's wearing a silk gown over a leotard. He makes a note of it: *She sleeps in an ivory gown printed with blue flowers and always forgets to turn off the light.* He can't be sure if she's already asleep. *She crosses over into sleep with barely a change in breath.* Ignacio imagines her dreams are as untroubled as he imagines her life. Is that something the immigration authorities would be interested in? The gulf between them?

He slips off his shoes and gets into bed. He's wearing a T-shirt and cotton pants, clothes he usually wears around the house. Underneath the pants, he wears a tight pair of briefs to hide his morning hard-on. Just in case.

Ignacio reads for a while by Maribel's light and then reaches over and turns it off. Maribel doesn't stir. She is his oldest friend in Miami. They met at a party that his cousin persuaded him to attend just three days after he arrived on a student visa. It was Maribel who took him to get a driver's license, Maribel who helped find him an apartment. Maribel always helped him, and Ignacio came to think of her as an older sister. When it became clear that he wasn't going to get citizenship on his own, his lawyer suggested that he get married. *I mean, assuming you're in love, I'm not suggesting you go and commit fraud, of course.* But Ignacio understood. The lawyer was recommended by a friend in the same situation as

Ignacio's, though in that case his friend decided to stay married after the game was up. Point is, Ignacio wouldn't be the first in his circle. But he couldn't think of anyone he genuinely wanted to marry. When he asked Maribel for advice, she immediately volunteered. Ignacio felt bad, as if he set the whole thing up, which he hadn't. He refused. But she insisted. And Ignacio finally accepted, graciously, only on the condition that she accept the going rate. She protested. *What kind of woman does that make me!* But in the end, she took the money, though she probably didn't need it. Ignacio realizes now, lying there in the night next to this woman, that he doesn't really know the important things about her. Maybe it was the same in all marriages. She told him once that she came to Miami in the crisis of '94, when she was thirty-three years old. But she's never told him about the trip itself. Ignacio doesn't know if they came on a homemade raft or if she paid someone to smuggle her. He doesn't know if she came alone or with family. Doesn't even know how many people were on the boat. Or if everyone survived. He knows nothing about her life in Holguín. And why is she a vegetarian anyway? He'd have to ask her all these things. He chastised himself. This was stuff he should already know. He felt like an irresponsible student cramming for an exam.

Ignacio turns onto his back and stares into the semidarkness. He is not sleepy. That thing that became dislodged in his chest is still knocking around. Its restlessness has infected him. Something changed today at lunch, when Maribel finally accepted. It wasn't just because Ignacio insinuated it was his investment on the line, not hers. Something else, maybe an eagerness. Whatever it was, Ignacio knows that he is not sufficiently aware to name it. When he tries to analyze it, the way he would any other problem, the feeling vanishes. But when he is resting, as he is now, off guard, with shadows gathering in the corners, it returns, an inner derangement that provokes in Ignacio a cold fear. It is in moments like this that Ignacio worries that he may not have outrun his father's madness.

He listens for Maribel's breathing. It is so light and so shallow it is as if he were sleeping next to a corpse. Ignacio turns to her. Not even the faintest stir. But when he accidently brushes her shoulder, he finds her skin moist and warm, as if her skin alone, of all her body, were still awake, watching him.

The thunder wakes Maribel—some presence has shaken her. She has always been afraid of lightning. As a girl, on the farm, they would remove all their jewelry and lie in bed until the storms passed. Years before, one of the field-workers was struck planting corn. The children were kept in the house, far from the sight of it. But Maribel has never been able to forget the smell of human flesh burning.

Ignacio is sleeping next to her. Maribel heard him when he came in last night. He fell asleep almost immediately after turning off her light. Maribel lay next to him, awake, for what seemed hours. At night, in the dark, this setup seems ridiculous. In the daytime she can make sense of the arrangement.

After all, they are far from the only ones. In Maribel's yoga studio an elderly lady confessed one evening that her own marriage to a much younger man was an act of charity so he could get his visa. Half the marriages in Miami are probably entered into for some utilitarian purpose or the other. How different is their arrangement from a couple who marries for health insurance, for example? Or because he wants a mother for his daughter? These are the things that Maribel thinks during the day. During the day it all seems very normal and acceptable. But then she wakes at night, as now, and the shadows loom. Everything seems headed for disaster. What the hell was she thinking? What the hell were they all thinking? At night, this seems like the absolute stupidest thing she's ever done. And where is the truth? Is reality the daytime Maribel or the nighttime Maribel?

Another flash, this one close. And then suddenly thunder explodes all around them, like the end of the world. Maribel grabs Ignacio's hand. It's an instinctive move, without thought, but also one that her mind has been practicing in the dark, hidden from her, these many months. Now, as if illuminated by a flash, she sees it plainly. Yes, of course, this was her desire from the start. Ignacio tightens his own hand around hers. She waits for him to speak. He is quiet. But she knows from his breathing that he is awake.

———

Ignacio tries to breathe normally. This night feels like a hex, like the soft inside of a glove you can't escape. He is irrational. Insane. His father's son. Already hard. The more he struggles against his hunger, the tighter it grips him. This woman beside him, this unknown element, draws him like the void. He can't remember such sharp pangs of desire, a desire stripped of tenderness or even want, a darkness that demands entry, no sense to it, no right or wrong, no past, no consequences, this is what it must be like to go mad, to give in to that thing you've been refusing to see, to surrender. Happiness and propriety be damned. I surrender, I surrender, murmurs Ignacio. And maybe Maribel hears him or maybe she doesn't, but at that moment, at the height of Ignacio's madness, she turns to him. And then they are a single, smooth-skinned serpent in the dark, all slippery-mouthed and eel-tongued. Lightning, with thunder right behind, hunting them all down.

===

The rain falls in heavy sheets all over Miami Beach that night. It falls on the Helena, on the soaked and exhausted strip of grass that encircles it, on the street, now resembling a river. It falls on the tops of the cars parked helplessly in the middle of the rising waters. No one has ever seen flooding like this. Rain falling on the tennis courts at Flamingo Park, on the palms that bend their fronds to let the water run, and on the flat roofs of dozens of apartments, a few of which, tonight, will develop a leak that will seem, at first, to be of little importance.

===

Ignacio wakes just after eight in the morning. Beatrice is not in her room. He stands at the threshold, taking it in. The bed undisturbed. This is how easy it is to throw your life away. He's always known it in theory. But he doesn't feel he had a choice in it either way. Not really: The attacks in New York, the storm last night, his own body over which he has so little control. Ignacio is overwhelmed by the forces that press from within and without. Biology is a kind of claustrophobia, he thinks, we cannot escape the prison of our senses, our absurd drives. Our need for other people.

In the bathroom, he runs the hot water. He stands under the stream a long time, enjoying the burn. He soaps his underarms, his chest, recalling the night, Maribel's scent . . . and now his cock half-hard in the suds, traitor. He walks to his room in just his towel—a first, as he has always dressed in the bathroom. He pulls on a fresh pair of shorts and a shirt and opens the blinds. The rain has stopped. The street probably flooded overnight: it's covered now with branches and bits of trash that must have floated free of the gutters.

Maribel is already in the kitchen. She looks up at him, as if waiting for his face before she arranges hers.

"I made coffee," she says.

"Thank you. Shall I go down for some pastelitos?" He smiles.

Maribel looks confused for a moment.

"Oh, right," she says. "Your ritual. Don't worry, I'll remember."

Ignacio takes a deep breath, "Look, Maribel, I—"

She holds up her hand, about to interrupt him, but then they both stop. The sound of keys in the door.

They look at one another. Beatrice steps into the living room. Her lipstick, Ignacio notes, is still perfect.

"Ah," she says. "I've interrupted the newlyweds."

Ignacio stands.

"What happened to you?" He tries to take her hands. "Where did you go?"

Beatrice pushes him gently away. "Nothing happened," she says. "The storm came through just as my shift was over. There was no way to get out—the lightning was fierce. So I stayed over with a friend."

A friend. It would be ridiculous for Ignacio to ask which friend. They're not adolescents and shows of jealousy are beneath him at this point. Especially in front of Maribel.

"Oh good," Ignacio says. "I was worried."

"I made some coffee," Maribel says.

"Sit, both of you," Ignacio says. "I'll make some French toast."

"Oh good," Beatrice says. "I'm starving. Take your time while I wash up."

AFTER BREAKFAST, THE THREE OF THEM LINGER around the dining room table as if they were roommates at university. Maribel turns on the Sunday talk shows—Beatrice and Ignacio have stopped complaining about them and Maribel assumes they've grown at least neutral to the chatter, though lately all the talk of war is becoming unbearable. Even on the morning shows: terrorism, terrorism, terrorism.

The hard knock at the front door makes all three of them jump. Maribel's eyes go wide.

"What on earth?"

Another knock. And after a moment: "Miami Beach police!"

Ignacio looks at the clock over the kitchen. His heart is thumping in his chest. This is it. This is it.

Another knock.

"Police. Anyone home?"

Maribel grabs his arm. "You have to tell them that Beatrice is the cleaning lady," she whispers.

"What?" Beatrice is standing. "I'm the cleaning lady now? Is that how it's going to be?"

"Shut up, both of you," Ignacio says.

Maribel pulls Ignacio's arm. "They'll deport the both of you, you don't understand."

"Shut up, Maribel. Let go of me. No one's going to get deported." Another knock at the door.

"Let me do the talking," Ignacio says. He pulls Maribel off his arm.

"Oh my god, oh my god," Maribel says.

Beatrice narrows her eyes at her. "Shut up and sit down."

Ignacio holds a finger to his lips as he opens the door. Two policemen stand there. One is tall and built, the other is short and fat and nodding.

"I'm Officer Duane, this is my partner, Frank. May we come in?"

Ignacio hesitates. "What is this about, Officers?"

Frank, the small one, steps inside first. "Don't worry," he says, and there is almost a smile on his lips. "None of you are in trouble. We just want to ask you a few questions about your neighbor."

"Neighbor?"

"Mrs. Alcalá."

The three of them look at one another.

"Did you know Mrs. Alcalá?"

Tears spring to Maribel's eyes. "Did? Is she . . . ?"

"No, no, she's fine," Frank says. "I should have said, *Do* you know Mrs. Alcalá?"

Ignacio shakes his head.

"Maybe . . . we've seen her . . ." He's always been ashamed about how little they know their neighbors here. When he was growing up, his mother knew all their neighbors and their neighbor's children. It suffocated him as a child; everyone knew their business and they knew everyone else's. But this . . . this didn't seem a better way to live.

"I'm sorry," he says. "We only moved in a little while ago and we . . . haven't met anyone."

"Right. Well, there was an attack last night. You didn't hear anything?"

Maribel's heart is pounding.

"An attack?"

"An assault," the cop says. "Unfortunately, the lady may lose her eye."

"Oh my god!"

"You didn't hear anything? Glass breaking?"

"There was a big storm," Maribel says. "A lot of thunder. But I feel like we would have heard some kind of attack."

Ignacio gives her a look.

"An assault? Was it a break-in? Was anything stolen?" Ignacio says.

"Not quite a break-in," Duane says. "Could have just been vandalism." He looks at Maribel again.

Maribel shakes her head. "Nothing. I—my husband and I—we were sleeping, and the only thing that woke me was the thunder, like I said."

"And you, miss?"

Beatrice shakes her head but says nothing.

"No one heard nothing," Frank says. "That's the way it these days. *See something, say something.* But no one sees nothing."

Ignacio expects them to leave after this, and Frank does look ready to go, but Duane, hand on his revolver, speaks directly to Ignacio.

"Any strange movements in the last few days that you can recall?"

"None that I can think of," Ignacio says. "To be honest, I can't be sure what she looks like . . . It's not a very tight-knit building."

"Shouting, anything like that?"

Ignacio shakes his head. "Nothing, I'm sorry. But the

storm was pretty violent. My god, this is awfully sad about Mrs. . . ." He's already forgotten the woman's name.

"Alcalá," Duane says.

"You never expect something like that in a building like this," Ignacio says.

Duane laughs. "Oh yeah? You never lived here in the eighties, I can tell."

The cops turn to leave.

"Yeah, well, thank you, Mr. and Mrs. Salas, for your time." Duane holds out his hand. Ignacio grows cold. How did they know his name?

"Please, come by if you need anything else," Ignacio says. The cops give him their business cards, in case something comes to him, in case he remembers anything about last night.

Ignacio slips the card into the back pocket of his jeans. Maribel grabs his hand. Together, they show the police to the door. After it shuts it behind them, Ignacio drops Maribel's hand.

Beatrice sits at the table, shaking. Ignacio kneels in front of her and envelopes her in his arms.

"I'm not leaving," Beatrice whispers.

───

Just past three that afternoon, Maribel fills the tub with the hottest water she can stand, not thinking, just listening to the violence of the water as it falls. When the tub is full, she dissolves two cups of Epsom salts. She strips, examines her thigh, passes her hand over the swelling welts. She lowers her body into the tub, wincing when raw skin meets the water. But numbness follows the initial shock of pain and Maribel can close her eyes.

After the cops left, she had to get out of the apartment. She changed into a bathing suit and walked out, leaving the front door open. She met the cops again in the hall—knocking on her next-door neighbor's door. The streets were slick and full of trash, but the sky was a clear blue, dotted here and there with white clouds, as if nothing had happened. She planned to walk for a bit along the shore, calm herself, as she'd always done, in contemplation of the sea, the sun, the sky, the clouds. Her mind was a chaos of feeling and she knew the water's tranquility would guide her back.

The sky overhead had cleared, but from the shore Maribel could see heavy clouds still obscuring the horizon. The beach seemed deranged; a village abandoned in a hurry. She struggled to find the romance in it but kept returning to evidence of desolation and decay: plastic tangled in the sargasso, juice boxes, straws, yogurt containers, a pink plastic hair roller. There weren't even any shells, only shards and rough stone. Maribel sat on the sand to practice her pranayama. Gusts of wind periodically kicked up sand and bits of plastic wrappers—the sky above may have recovered, but the world below, which once seemed composed of peaceful order and hidden symmetry, revealed itself now in all its unpredictable treachery.

She sat on the shore for a few minutes, breathing, trying not to think. The clouds shifted over the sun and suddenly cast the beach in a strange orange glow. Maribel had never seen anything like it. She tossed off her dress and walked into the sea, remembering the knowing glance between Ignacio and Beatrice, the dropped hand. She waded in until the water reached her shoulders. She turned a somersault in the water and then another. And just as she was about to come out, she felt a powerful current that nearly toppled her. The force of it hit her thigh and then her stomach. She moved her arm to scare whatever it was away, and a thin tentacle slashed her upper arm as well. The pain made her cry out the whole long way to the shore. Within seconds, the white skin of her stomach and thigh was crisscrossed by thick red lacerations.

She returned to the apartment to find Beatrice and Ignacio at the kitchen table. Both laughing and sharing a bottle of wine.

"I'm going to take a bath," she'd said. "Unless anyone needs the bathroom in the next hour."

"Okay," Ignacio said. "Go ahead. We're good."

"Yeah, we're good," Beatrice repeated.

The apartment is between tenants again. It is midnight on a Wednesday night in the middle of the month, in the middle of the year.

The curtains are drawn, the lights are out. The air conditioner—which must remain on all summer to fight the mold—cycles on at regular intervals. When the motor clicks off, other sounds take over: a car alarm, distant music, a man's voice yelling, "Fucking balls!" Sometimes the motor stops and there seems to be no sound left to take its place. But it's only that the ears have dulled, listen carefully: A distant cricket, the hum of other air conditioners, the rustle of palm fronds. The motor cycles on again. The machine roaring away, as if it were a living thing doing battle with the heat. No one here to witness its courage. The following cycle reveals the sound of scurrying. While the rooms wait for their next inhabitants, its other, more numerous citizens come forth to enjoy the delights of apartment 2B.

A white mouse dashes across the uneven floor of the kitchen. Tap, tap, tap, its nails like tiny high heels in a hurry. The air conditioner switches on and the mouse stops. Only the nose twitches. After a moment, he continues. Out the kitchen and quickly into the living room. He stands for a second, crouched, listening, his small imagination filled with a thousand fears. He doesn't last very long out in the open. Another second and he's hurried off again, this time beneath the couch. But there is another mouse, now leaving the bathroom. This one is a little bigger, a little fatter, more self-confident. He hurries, but also takes long pauses before he moves again. He jogs along the baseboards, seems about to climb on a credenza left behind, and then reverses. Back on the floor, he pauses, hears something, and then shoots back, dashing across the room and into a hole in the kitchen cabinets.

One fat roach crawls out of the sink drain, pauses, and then scrambles over the rim. Up the wall, and then under the cabinets. The streetlight catches him at an angle, elongating his shadow and exaggerating the length of his six furiously moving legs. Two more roaches, these smaller, crawl out of the drain behind him. They scatter in opposite directions, like spies on a pointless mission. When the air-conditioning cycles off again, the silence opens to reveal the sound of the mice, returned to their base beneath the roof. From the corner formed where the refrigerator meets the counter, there drops another, more delicate shadow. It sways beneath the night light, centimeters from the countertop: a spider, all patience and spindle-legged elegance. She hovers for a moment before hauling herself back up.

Dawn, at last, and the apartment returns to itself. But something remains. A heaviness fills the empty rooms. Beyond the walls, the muffled sound of weeping and a piano's lonely notes.

PILAR, 2010

Pilar pulls the tape across the top and seals the last box. Books. It's taken the move for her to realize that most of what she owns is in words. Thirteen boxes of books, five boxes of kitchen stuff, three wardrobe-style boxes of clothes (she's already gotten rid of most of her work clothes) and one box of office supplies, most of them stolen over the years from the *Horror*. Words, words, words. Words in the mail, "You owe blah blah blah." Words on Facebook, that flash-in-the-pan her editors made her sign up for. Words on Twitter, *Outrageous!* followed by a stupid link that she'll click anyway. What's the point of it? What did all the books give her? She's forgotten most of what she's read. And, anyway, it's no way to make a living. Even less so now when every jackass is a "citizen journalist." Her mother warned her twenty years ago. Pilar hates to admit she was right.

So, this is it. Pilar sits on a box of hardcovers. Her life in twenty-two boxes. Pilar is being melodramatic, fuck it. She's forty years old and she's moving back in with her parents. She can be as maudlin about it as she likes.

The real estate lady just left, shutting the door softly on apartment 2B. Anna something or other, but not Cuban. Pilar signed all the forms without reading them. Her brother (*my son the doctor*, as her mother refers to him) is coming by in an hour to help her haul most of this junk to storage. And tonight, she'll sleep in her old bedroom in her parents' house. Next Monday, someone else, someone she has never met, will start living in her apartment for $1,900 a month—the best income, even after maintenance and taxes—that she's seen in more than a year.

Pilar is a victim of the *financial crisis*—a term she abhors, really, mostly because in its anxiety to appear inoffensive, it reminds her of herself. Financial crisis. Everyone repeats it as if it were a perfectly acceptable term for the soul-mangling, no-turning-back, fucking utter disaster that ruined her life.

Pilar's the worst offender, she admits it. She's lost count of how many times she's used that stupid phrase in cover letters. "After the financial crisis, I took stock of my talents and . . ." Or: "Following the financial crisis, I decided to reinvent myself as a . . ." Blah blah blah. All desperate nonsense that nobody bought—least of all, Pilar. Words. She had no illusions. She was a reporter for almost twenty years. One unfortunate side effect of such a long internment is that your capacity for your own bullshit becomes severely constrained. The truth—the harsh no-holds-barred reality—is that Pilar is a loser. She was trained to see things plainly and now she cannot turn away from herself. She has lost at the game of life.

What's worse is that even in her suffering, she can make no claim to greatness. Hers is not a particularly interesting or original story. Earlier this year, after eighteen years with *The Miami Horror* (which HR decided to calculate down to eight years because of an ill-advised leave that she took in 2001 cuando se enfermó de los nervios), Pilar was *involuntary separated*. Involuntary separation. That's what they call *fired* now. Lord Jesus why aren't people rioting in the streets to defend the English language? But so it goes: an institution that so long trafficked in precise language, at least when it came to the suffering of others, took refuge in corporate babble when it came to reckoning with its own crimes. *Involuntary separation.* Her editor gave her the news over the phone. Two days later, she was signing a "certificate of separation," which included a clause stipulating that in return for her laughable hush money ($18,000 after taxes) she promised not to trash her idiotic former employers. Fuck them. But she signed.

The enormity of it didn't hit her at once. Pilar assumed she would be able to find a job elsewhere. Over the years, she'd received many offers from distant suitors: *The Washington Post*, the *Los Angeles Times*. And she'd always turned them down (though not before extracting a nice raise from the *Horror* in the process). Pilar is Cuban, Miami-born; Miami—for better or worse, usually worse—is home. She went to elementary and high school here, parochial schools. She graduated from college here. She got her first job here. Her entire family is here: seven cousins, eight aunts and uncles, two sets of grandparents, one still living. A thousand friends and acquaintances. Memories of hurricanes: some vicious, some empty threats. Swap shop, Westchester Mall, el ten-cent, Lourdes Academy, enormous steaks at El Cristo, Luria's, Europa Shoes, MDCC. Pilar cannot conceive of living anywhere else.

For several months after her firing, Pilar lived in dreamland. She continued her Wednesday ritual of lunch at Books & Books and kept up her Saturday night visits to Duffy's, secure in the delusion that she was still wanted. As summer turned to fall, reality began to intrude on her idyll. Which is to say, Pilar began to run out of money.

Pilar sent out a few résumés and emails. But after eighteen years as an investigative reporter in Miami, the last two as a columnist, she'd managed to piss off every major employer in town. Working for the county was out, of course, as was the city of Miami. Same went for the University, Tetra Associates, the Tanar Group, Bonarts. The list was depressingly long.

She wrote a few magazine articles ("How to Tell if Your Man Is Lying to You") that kept her afloat for a while. She tried writing for one of those internet mills (lasted half a day). Most recently, she'd landed an adjunct position at a community college in North Broward. The pay barely covered gas money. After taxes and maintenance on the condo, she was in the red. And she didn't have health insurance. Something had gone wrong in this country between the time she graduated from high school and the time she found herself in middle age, broke and without prospects. What was it exactly? Where had they all failed one another?

As a columnist she was paid to know, or at least pretend to know. She wrote angry columns, funny columns, boring columns. Every one of them filled with the certainty of the second-rate. Her ex-husband, that London-born worm, had a bunch of British sayings and that was his favorite, supposedly originating as a dig at Margaret Thatcher, of whom some wag had remarked: "She has the certainty of the second-rate." Her ex never used this one to her face, but she can imagine him applying it to her now. Yes, Pilar will be honest with herself. She has a second-rate intelligence. Why else would she have married that serial two-timing jackass? Why else would she be in the mess she is now?

Certainty. Bush was certain that Afghanistan was worth invading. She was certain it was not. Bush was certain that capitalism would save the world. She was certain it would not. But even as she wrote her columns, she had her doubts. *No one wants to read about your doubts!* her editor shouted at her. But why not? Why couldn't one have doubts and express them publicly? Why couldn't she say now, for all the world to read, that she doesn't know what went wrong with America in the years between her adolescence and middle age? How is it that her parents, just ten years after their arrival, were able to send two children to private school, own a home, drive two cars, and vacation on the beach every summer for three weeks? In those early years, before they both struck it rich in their careers, did her parents ever worry about health insurance? Not that she can remember. Were they just shielding Pilar and her brother from hard realities? Unlikely, as her father's specialty was creating and wallowing in communal anxiety.

So, what was it? Was it really Reagan's fault—all those unfortunates he abandoned to the streets? Or was it Clinton and his easy mortgages? Now that no one is paying her for her opinion, Pilar can admit that she doesn't really have one, that the air went out of her long ago. It's all too complicated, beyond her sorting. All she knows for certain now is that someone really fucked her over.

So Pilar has made the decision. She will move back in with her parents—temporarily!—and rent out this cucarachera that she and her husband bought for a mere $80,000 in 2003, when the building went condo. Three years later, just in time for her divorce, this dump had been appraised at $350,000. In the first of what would be a series of stupid financial moves, Pilar bought out her ex-husband, with the neat little result that in 2010 she finds herself, like every other surviving stooge in South Beach, owing more on the apartment than it is worth. Forget the fancy language of the agents. Here's the deep structure of the Florida real estate market: It is nothing more than a two-million-strong game of hot potato. First the prices start rising. Then developers of new construction hire trapeze artists and dancing elephants. Then your uncle tells you about a friend who has a cousin whose orthodontist bought a condo on Friday for $40,000 and flipped it on Monday for $600,000. And you're the poor idiot who buys the condo for $600,000, expecting it to double in value in a week, and then, boom. You're left holding what we'll politely call the soft, smelly, steaming spud. This happened to a lot of people. Pilar certainly wasn't the only one. Hers wasn't even the worst case; it only seems like it to Pilar. Some people walked away from the bad debt. Just stopped paying. But Pilar isn't built like that. She comes from solid northern Spanish stock. Peasants who prided themselves on a kind of high-minded thriftiness that hasn't been spotted in the United States since the Dutch founded Manhattan. When her mother's parents arrived in Miami in 1965, they already held doctorates in financial fuckups. From damp outhouses in Galicia, they traveled to Cuba on steerage in the early twentieth century, and in thirty years built fortunes being the nastiest bunch of penny-pinching grocers the island had ever known. Their refusal to pay for anything they could do themselves, their insistence on resoling a single pair of shoes to last them a lifetime, their horror of buying anything new or at full price, made them exotic anywhere in the realms of late capitalism—doubly so in the America of self-helped optimism. But Pilar's parents and uncles and grandparents knew that money never lasts. That forces beyond your control can quickly conspire to rob you of a very nice pension. They took one look at the free-spending Americans and instantly understood the secret workings of the U.S. economy. "With frugal campesinos like us," declared one uncle, "this country would never progress."

PILAR'S PLAN IS TO RENT OUT THE APARTMENT and net a little extra cash each month while she plots her next move. Never mind the walls are, like literally, made of paper, that mice overrun the place, that neighbors don't talk to one another, and that an actual, real-life madman lives below: The place photographs nice. Typical South Beach. But for this plot to work, of course, she would have to find a way to live rent-free. Like countless other Gen-Xers, she has opted to move back in with her parents. It was an obvious choice, of course. Her father, now retired, had been a vice president for an international medical equipment firm. Her mother is a locally known fashion designer who still lends her name to a line of jewelry sold first at Richard's, then Burdines, and, for now at least, Macy's.

These days, they live in upper-middle-class splendor in Coral Gables, right on the golf course. Her parents bought the house for cash during one of Miami's many burst bubbles and never tired of wowing visitors with the low price they paid. The house has six rooms and four baths, plus an extra room, bath, and small kitchen in the maid's quarters over the garage. There's never been a maid in it, only Pilar's grandmother. Her parents have a Salvadoran woman come in once a week to do the cleaning. A live-in maid is considered a needless extravagance. Exile long behind them, they could well afford the kind of cars their neighbors drive, but they insist on their Hondas. They're worth several million over, but, aside from the house, you'd never know it. Most days, you'll find Pilar's dad working on the yard in his torn chinos and frayed T-shirts—most of them cast-offs from Pilar's 5K races. He'll forget how he's dressed and drive right to Publix in his lawn-boy getup. The people stare. He doesn't notice. An obviously comfortable, stress-free old age, something Pilar will never see.

Marco is knocking at Pilar's door. She breathes in once, twice. She waits a moment. She must be sure to put on her best smile.

Her parents wanted Pilar to be a lawyer, naturally. A doctor would have been better, but they figured early on she didn't have the head or stomach for it. One of the most disappointing days in their lives was when she told them that she was going to be a journalist.

"In Cuba, the lowest people were the journalists," said her mother.

"The job won't even cover the price of gas," said her father.

But now that she's moving back with them, they're finally happy. Cuban parents aren't like American parents. They like having their kids near, proximity being conducive to the kind of micromanaging parenting style they prefer. Pilar's brother lived with them all through medical school, a *brilliant* financial decision that their parents, more than twenty years later, still find occasion to praise. Pilar teased him for that mercilessly over the years, so when weighing the decision to move back into their parents' house, the thought that gave her the most pause was what Marco would say. Pilar and her brother have a good enough rapport now, maintained by distance. But Marco has always been the typical oldest child, and typical Cuban son. Pilar became a feminist in 1985, when her mother, paying no matter to the fact that Pilar was lying on the couch blissfully engrossed in a book, asked her to make her brother a sandwich. "Pobrecito," her mother called from her work room. The *pobrecito* was tired after football practice. And that's how it always went. Marco was *pobrecito* and Pilar had *malas pulgas*.

Pilar opens the door and kisses her brother. She smiles as genuinely as she can.

"So all right," Marco says, "let's do this. Glad you're getting out of this creepy dump."

Marco helps her load her things onto the truck. They make four trips, and on the fifth, Pilar, exhausted, drops the big living room lamp and it shatters. Almost instantly comes the shouting from below.

"Knock it off, bitch!"

Without pausing to consider anything, Pilar stomps her foot three times, boom boom boom!

"You knock it off, asshole! Keep it up and I'll rent this place to a circus troupe!"

"Calm down," Marco tells her.

"Guy's a fucking maniac," she says. "I'm sick of him."

When all the boxes are gone, Pilar closes the door behind her without looking back.

"Did you find a tenant?" her brother says once they're on the highway.

"The agent did," Pilar says. "Some recent arrival."

"Oh?"

"Some Cuban. Lenin García."

"Lennon?" her brother asks. "As in, 'Can't Buy Me Love'?"

"No. Lenin," Pilar says. "As in, 'Capitalism is fascism in decay.'"

"Sounds like a misquote."

"Just because it never happened doesn't mean it isn't true," Pilar says. "Anyway, what do I care about misquotes? I'm not a reporter."

Armando is the part-time building manager, who has come to apartment 2B to let in the cleaners. He leans against the window-sill to wait. He saw the boy on the stairs once or twice, but he didn't really talk to him. It's the same everywhere you go in this country. No one really knows anyone else; no one knows your private life. That's why no one could tell you anything about the young man. You look at the mailboxes in this building, the names: Russian, Arab, French, Spanish. Every kind of person lives in Miami, but mostly they know only their kind of person. It's as if they were all lantern slides, each shining its own light. The Cubans, they're not the biggest group, but they take up a lot of space. They're the ones most likely to talk about everything they lost. The older ones, they want to talk about the island. At first Armando thought he would just tell them he was born there. But that would be difficult—he would have to memorize realistic details, and someone would know it was just a story . . . Armando doesn't have anything to hide. He's lived an honorable life. It's simply easier, in Miami, to be Cuban. But not everyone understands that. If they discovered Armando was not what he said, they would assume bad things. It could be unpleasant for them and for Armando. He realized it would be better to say that he was not born there, but his parents were. This is true of many people in Miami anyway. So Armando looked at a map and picked the smallest, most lonely village. That will be funny, the day he meets someone from Baracoa . . . He probably

should have just said "la Habana" like everyone else. Then it might not be so strange if no one knew his parents there. Armando imagines Baracoa is some place like Bazgir . . . everyone is related in some way . . . So now he hopes he doesn't meet anyone from Baracoa . . . Armando is not a criminal. He's not hiding under a new identity. He is an American hero. This is a funny title to him. He also laughs at it himself. American hero . . . but it's true. That is how he is here, with all the papers, and a good job managing five different buildings in South Beach, even if he can't afford to live in any of them, yet. Arman Latifi was born a year after the Soviet invasion. Whole life of war. No men left in the villages. Can any American imagine this? War made them a country of orphans and cripples. And still they continued! Armando also, no mother, no father. But at least he did not see them murdered with his own eyes, as so many did . . . Only one brother left, he stays now in Pakistan, but Armando is trying to bring him. Inshallah, next year. His family is Tajik, not Pashtun. Americans don't know the difference. But the Tajiks fought the Taliban—Armando is always tempted to explain this. The great leader Massoud, who would have finished the Taliban, he was murdered the day before September eleventh. That is why nobody remembers him . . . he was just one death. But the Tajiks mourned Ahmad Shah Massoud the way they mourned family. For a long time, people said he had not died . . . that he was playing a trick to ambush the Pashtun . . . Maybe this is true. Maybe Massoud is not dead. Armando's brother, he worked as an interpreter for the U.S. also, but his English was not as good as Armando's. No one believes him, but Armando did not go to school for his English. No, he learned it from BBC radio. And then when

he met his first Americans, they had no idea what he was saying!
But American English is easier. Armando learned it very quickly.
He went everywhere. He saw his country for the first time. He
saw bodies . . . babies' bodies. He saw so many things. So many
many ugly things. For that whole first year Armando could not
sleep, remembering. One time, he was with the soldiers in a con-
voy through the Desert of Death, this is a true name, and there is
nothing, nothing, nothing until they come to a small village and
a little boy comes running . . . Maybe four years old . . . maybe a
refugee. Thinking big noisy trucks are for candy, not killing . . .
this boy, he comes running, and behind, his mother screaming and
everyone on the truck screaming. Armando is screaming, Stop! Ist!
Wadrega! Ruken! in every language he knows, but the little boy, he
keeps coming, and after the first explosion, Armando looks away.
He covers his face with his scarf, crying . . . But his country . . .
Armando's country is beautiful in spite of all things. Not beautiful
like here. Here is a place of blues and greens. There, everything
is brown, but the mountains, when the sun is rising, there is no
vision like that. It is a vision of God . . . Armando has lived in
Miami Beach for four years. The first time he realized he would
have hot water every day, whatever time he wanted, that was like
a festival! But then soon he forgot about the water, like everyone
else. His grandmother, who raised them, used to say that no one
needs time to get used to good things . . . But Armando did need
time. The first year alone was very difficult. No friends. The people
here . . . they are not like his people. Where he's from, everyone is
invited inside for tea and pistachios, strangers, too. But when Ar-
mando invited some of the neighbors in his building for tea, they

said, No, thank you. Armando was lonely for a long time. But his religion does not allow despair. Hope—hope comes from God.

If only Armando could have talked to this young man before . . . If only he had stopped him one time on the stairs. Ist! Wadrega! Ruken! Always the warnings come too late. Tomorrow, Armando will return with flowers—white roses, for forgiveness—and he will set them on the threshold in memory of this boy, of poor Lenin García.

LENIN, 2011

A nna Kralova stands outside the door, listening. This irrational impulse makes her cringe, though she knows no one is here to record her embarrassment. Anna does not believe in ghosts. She believes that when we die, we are gone forever. She believes everything we know of the world, we know through our senses, a sudden flaming vision through time. And yet how to explain this feeling? This sense of a foreign sadness that's been lodged in her throat since the young man's death.

She turns her key in the lock. Not too slowly, not too quickly. As naturally as she can, she opens the door to apartment 2B. The door swings into silence. What was she expecting? Creaking hinges? A cold spot on the floor? Footsteps? Anna smiles to herself. For days afterward, that odious man downstairs continued to complain about phantom footfalls.

There is no one here. There is nothing here. Just Anna and her breathing. The apartment is vacant. But vacant in a way that Anna has never experienced. More of a gray absence. The little rooms, the bare kitchen cabinets all speak now of a place hollowed of life. And the faint antiseptic clinging to the air is itself a kind of ghost, a reminder of what happened here.

Anna Kralova didn't know much about the tenant beyond his name, Lenin García, and that he recently arrived from Cuba. She met him only twice, at the showing and when he came into the office to sign the lease. The man downstairs was a problem since day one—Lenin called her office at least once a week to complain.

When the police called Anna to relay the news, the first thing she thought was that the downstairs neighbor had shot Lenin dead. But it was *just a suicide*, the police said. One of many in this town. The policewoman, in a kind voice, said she was sorry—an English construction Anna had never been able to accept. What was there to be sorry about? As if the bad that happened always had to be someone's fault.

As soon as Anna hung up, she called the owner. Pilar was a former reporter with not a hair's worth of sentimentality. She told Anna not to worry, that she would handle everything, and they'd put the place up for rent "straightaway." Before hanging up, Pilar added, "It won't affect anything. We don't have to disclose it."

Ghosts were trickier, less disposed to discretion. And just to be safe, the owner suggested, Anna might want to light some sage. Anna assumed it was in jest. But then she was at Target and there, in the bargain bin, as if an ancient trickster were calling her by name, sat a big green sage candle.

Now Anna takes the candle out of her purse and sets it on

the counter. The first match she strikes is humid. The second one is weak, but Anna manages to light the wick before the match goes out. The candle flame sputters, threatens to extinguish, and then flares with such ferocity that Anna takes a step back.

——

Anna was seventeen when the wall fell. Two years later, she was working for the Ministry of Foreign Affairs. Over the years, her parents sold off pieces of jewelry, china, even the silverware her grandparents hid after the war, to pay for English lessons for their only daughter. Later, those lessons benefitted the entire family. It helped that Anna was pretty. But what got her into the foreign ministry was her flawless English, acquired clandestinely from an elderly British lady whose pedagogy involved memorizing long passages of English poetry.

In the early years after the revolution, Prague, like the rest of Eastern Europe, was awash in suitors: corporate, national, international. Anna worked fifteen-hour days, going from meeting to meeting as interpreter. She accepted the job instead of going to college. She couldn't have hoped for a better course in international business. Anna heard pitches from car companies, fast-food businesses, chocolate empires, all the time wondering at this new kind of twisted poetry. She understood the individual words but couldn't make sense of the sentences they strung together. "If we can leverage this synergy, the impact on your market will be off the charts." But slowly she came to understand. And though she would never say this to anyone, she overcame the translation hurdles by assuming that these Western apparatchiks were using language in the same way her own had done all her life. After that it became easy: substitute one nonsense phrase in English for its equivalent in Czech.

One evening, she sat in a conference room with her bosses and the representatives from USAID. Three men on their side, three men on hers. By this time, Anna had already met many Americans, but they never failed to impress. So healthy-looking, with their straight white teeth, their shiny hair. Cheeks gone pink in the lingering spring cold. And, of course, the smiles. She had yet to meet an American who didn't smile. She was still another year away from her first trip to the Midwest. But already she imagined a country full of men and women like this, shiny with wealth's good humor.

In contrast, her own people. "Beaten down by history," as her grandmother always said, with her usual abundance of drama. And maybe she was right. What did these brand-new Americans know of war or occupation? Did they even know what it was to be hungry?

The meeting started with the usual preliminaries. The Americans asked after her bosses' families, something they must have learned in a seminar somewhere. It was a tick that always made Anna recoil, as if a guest opened the refrigerator in her home without permission. After the preliminary nonsense, the men wandered down to the discussion. Her bosses understood English very well, but they still let her handle the interpreting. That way they couldn't be blamed—that much hadn't changed.

The Americans were there to talk about entrepreneurship and markets. The conversation went back and forth. They offered their expertise. The bosses always made a big, elaborate show of gratitude, obviously faked to Anna's eyes, but they must have known the Americans were a willing audience for this kind of thing: *We are so very grateful, so much work is still needed, our country is so far behind Western-style development.* The Americans always cheered to this kind of talk, promising they *could cover infrastructure costs*, ensure there weren't *too many stumbles on the road to privatization.*

After an hour of this, Anna's boss turned to her and said, in Czech, "Look, dearie, don't translate what I'm about to tell you. But can you speed this up a bit? We just want their money."

═══

Anna takes a few steps and stops, suddenly cold. Sharp knocking comes through the floor. Then a shaky voice cries up through the wood slats, "Knock it off!"

Christ. That nasty man. She stomps once on the floor in anger, then slips off her heels. After a moment, she takes the camera out of its case, pops in the wide-angle. The investigation took a little more than a month. When it was over, Anna arranged to have the young man's possessions removed, though when she steps into the kitchen, she sees that—typical Miami—the workers did the job imperfectly: A cast-iron pan sits on the stove. And, opening the doors beneath the sink, Anna finds a purple bottle of Fabuloso next to a dented canister of Comet.

Anna stashes the cast-iron pan beneath the sink with the supplies and steps back to take a photo, angling the shot so the dent in the floor is not visible. The light is good. She takes a few more shots, satisfied. But when Anna checks the view screen, every photo she's taken of the kitchen is framed by grotesque shadows. She extinguishes the silly sage candle and starts over. The small living room, the bathroom. The smaller bedroom the owner used as an office. She leaves the main bedroom for last. Anna hesitates at the threshold. The refinished floor is dark and shiny, unmarred.

She takes a deep breath and steps into the room. He slit his wrists. Just twenty-one years old. He slit his wrists until all the blood drained from him. A friend found him. Or a client—the police later told Anna that Lenin worked as a prostitute. Her immediate reaction was to protest, as if it were her duty to preserve the honor of the dead. "He was a masseuse!" she cried. The cops laughed.

Anna crouches for a shot of the closet. Walk-in closets, even small ones, are rare in buildings of this age. That will be a nice *selling point*, as her broker would say. Anna is closing the doors again when she notices something—a shadow—on the top shelf. She stops. A yellow box pushed back against a corner. She taps the light switch. A suitcase. Anna considers the situation. The suitcase might belong to one of the painters. Or even to Armando. Perhaps, Anna thinks, the manager stayed a few nights, unable to resist the temptation of a new home, new sheets, a different life.

Anna clings to this version for as long as she can. But her life has accustomed her to seeing things clearly. No worker would have left a suitcase here. Armando would never risk his job. Still Anna does not move. Someone else will remove the suitcase. Anna closes the closet doors. She begins to walk away. She will send someone, maybe one of the same workers. If it was his suitcase, he will be glad for the opportunity to take it home. And if it belonged to the dead man, someone will throw it away. Anna pictures the yellow suitcase lying in the Dumpster outside. And what of the boy's family? Wouldn't Anna, living far from home and all alone, wish a stranger to gather the small evidence of her life? Isn't that part of the respect we owe the dead?

Anna opens the closet again. The suitcase is a solid thing, a mute invitation. She stands on tiptoe and nudges it side to side until a corner hangs over the edge. Anna grabs and yanks hard. But the suitcase is lighter than she expects, and it flies across the room, landing with a crash before bursting open. Papers are still flying down when violent tapping echoes through the room. Anna's heart seizes. Then the disembodied voice from below, "Knock it off!"

Jesus, Mary, and Joseph. Anna is afraid to move. Papers litter the room. Slowly, quietly, she gathers them. Receipts, letters, photographs. She sorts them in piles. Lodged into the corner of the suitcase, a brick of letters, tightly wound in rubber bands. Anna releases them and the letters fall open, dozens, all written on airmail paper. Long letters in a tiny script. Almost all of them begin with *Gracias por el dinero, mi hijo.* Anna's Spanish is not perfect, but she can read most of it, at least understand their meaning. *Me alegro mucho. Que bonita suerte. Como te estraño.* All the words a mother would write. About happiness and longing and the good luck that her son was enjoying in an abundant land. How pleased she was that he was making a life for himself, however much it hurt that he was so far away.

Anna sits with the suitcase for a long time, much longer than she expected, absorbed in the story unfolding page by page. She finds other letters, from friends, perhaps. A birthday card, handmade from pressed paper, a bird in flight has wings that open and close like a fan. A pile of medical receipts. The results of an HIV test—negative. A Cuban passport, the photo in black-and-white of an impossibly young man. Some two dozen photographs of young people, smiling at the shore, in the fields, on the lawn of what seems to be a park, or a cemetery.

It seems so long ago that Anna landed in this city. How little she knew then. Spirits press down on her, and again and again she rejects them. Sends them packing, back to the pre-rational past. Not a haunting, but an echo. The boy's life a gesture pointing back to her own. A dream of a thousand iterations. From nowhere, now, comes a fragment of Yeats, a ghostly melody.

I would spread the cloths under your feet:
But I, being poor, have only my dreams;
I have spread my dreams under your feet;
Tread softly because you tread on my dreams.

═══

Maybe her father was right, maybe she never should have left. Now she is neither American nor Czech. Now she is some in-between thing, diminished.

"I was in Prague after the split," Pilar told her after they signed the rental lease with Lenin. "I loved it."

"Yes," Anna said. "Americans love Prague."

Pilar nodded. "Because of Kafka, probably."

Of course, Kafka and the Charles Bridge. The extent of American knowledge of Prague. How could Anna explain that she hadn't even read Kafka until she moved to the U.S.? Thanks to her eccentric education, she knew more about Shakespeare and Auden, could recite long passages from Yeats many years before she made the acquaintance of Gregor Samsa.

So much time gone by. Anna grasps at the blurred edges of her childhood, the past no longer the certain shelter she imagined for herself. Is it like this for everyone, or only for those who leave? The loss of her childhood language, the acquisition of a new one, altered the topography of memory. Her poor, lonely mother tongue has run out of stories to tell. And the present is a tyrant who only speaks English. *I am old with wandering through hollow lands and hilly lands . . .*

How long since her last trip home? Three years? Five. Yes, it's been five years since she stood at the Palacký Bridge, tracing the Vltava's black embroidery through the city, five years since she sat with her mother over a cup of tea and talked for hours about her old friends: who made it, who didn't, who got out, who stayed behind.

When she was a girl, her parents visited her mother's village in Slovakia every summer. Today the trip takes less than five hours. But in those days, it was almost a full day's journey in their old Škoda, from eight in the morning to five in the evening. They usually stayed for two weeks, setting back early on the morning of departure. But one year, they didn't leave the village until late afternoon. Night caught them on the road. They moved through the darkened countryside, the rocking and steady hum of the car lulling Anna in and out of sleep. As they approached Bratislava, a great glow came up behind the hills. It was as if the moon had fallen to earth.

Anna's father must have seen her pressing her face to the glass.

"That's Vienna," he said.

"The lights of the city," murmured her mother.

Vienna, city of great lights. And for the rest of Anna's childhood, that's what the unreachable West felt like, an otherworldly radiance set in the wilderness, a place where people refused to give in to the natural gloom.

The memory loosens others. They come rushing back to Anna in her native tongue. A to je ta krásná země, země česká domov můj. Her skinny schoolgirl years. A boy she loved.

The first smell of summer. The lovely childhood lived in quiet obedience. And how the end of it—the protests, the thousands in the square—all tasted to her of love. That's what it was like to live inside great changes, to ache for a life viewed so long from a distance.

She's lived in Miami for nine years. Three years before that in Chicago. Two years in Los Angeles. Almost half her life in a foreign country. Though it doesn't feel like a foreign country. The foreign country is here, Anna thinks. She is the foreign country. So many years finding homes for strangers. How many people had she met? She's lost track. She can't remember all of them, though it occurs to her that each may remember her, lit up against the blazing hope of a new life, the desire that delivered them to her.

Who will remember Lenin García? How did he get here? How long had he been dreaming of Miami? Anna knows almost nothing of his story. But she knows that he left his home before dawn so his mother would not see his tears. Knows that the sadness of leaving was mixed with an electric anticipation no one who has never left can understand. No, Anna does not believe in ghosts; we are our own ghosts, dragging our mournful pasts behind us forever.

Anna repacks the suitcase, taking her time. She refolds the letters and secures them with the rubber band. She stacks the certificates, the birthday card. She gathers the photographs into a pile, the strangers still laughing by the foreign sea, sweetly mocking Anna Kralova, a woman they don't even know exists. After she folds the last page, Anna closes the suitcase and sits with her head in her hands.

History seems like a big thing to those outside of it. But it's experienced in miniature: a boat's humid hold, a creased passport, a small suitcase full of papers dragged from city to city. Nemoc na koni přijíždí a pěšky odchází. So much lost between languages, forgotten in transit. So many dreams in this town. Miscommunications and galloping misfortunes. It was her grandmother's favorite phrase, uttered in every season: misfortune arrives on horseback and departs on foot. Her grandmother, who survived three currencies and witnessed both the crushed Spring and the fall of the wall. Now she is buried in a city of Zara and Starbucks, a Prague she would scarcely recognize.

Anna will see about the papers. Maybe she will track down Lenin's mother. Someone always lives long enough to collect the photographs. Someone, somewhere, will find meaning in the fragments now floating free of the life that sustained them.

After a long while, Anna stands, legs shaking, and rolls the suitcase across the floor as quietly as she can.

Seven in the morning. Reina knocks on the door to apartment 2B and the manager lets her in. As usual, she's the first to arrive. Magda and Rosario will come at nine with the vacuum cleaner. The Realtor asked them not to start until ten, but Reina promised they wouldn't make noise. By ten, she'll be on to her next house.

She sets the bag with her cleaning things inside. She flips the switch by the door. Good. At least there is still electricity. The Realtor didn't tell her about the suicide, but Magda, que se entera de todo, *told her the whole story. Anyway, what's another dead body to a woman from San Pedro Sula? Phantoms don't scare Reina. The world as we know it already holds horrors enough. Reina doesn't believe in the supernatural. She believes in work. She is built for it, like her father was: short and wide and strong.*

Reina has been cleaning houses since she arrived in Miami three years ago. Never mind how she got here. Or her real name. In her circle, most people mind their own business. That's one thing she likes about this city. The rest of it, she doesn't think about. On the bus, the smelly people, their empty eyes. The drip in the kitchen she shares with five others. The roaches. The rats scratching their claws into the ceiling at night. She doesn't think about it. No good, so much thinking. It gets in the way of work. And work keeps her busy, which keeps her from thinking. Which is a good thing when you're a mother who left her baby in the most violent city on earth.

Joaquin, five years old in August. Each month, Reina sends *back $500, some months she can manage $600. Three months ago, someone started following her son and his grandmother around San Pedro, asking questions. So Reina sent the last months' cash through three different agencies. Next month, she hopes to send it with a friend who is returning. In her last phone call to her mother, Reina spoke plainly: Don't buy expensive clothes, don't do anything to the house. Don't draw any attention, that's how you survive in this life. Don't talk about your fortune or misfortune. Don't talk about the sums that come your way. Don't let anyone know where I am. Better to tell them I am dead, she told her mother. The money is for food and for Joaquin's education, that's it.*

Joaquin, not even five, and he can already read. He is very clever. Reina sends him letters, which he reads out loud to his grandmother. And last month, for the first time, he wrote back to her. Mamá, te quiero. Handwriting still shaky, but sure. Reina keeps the note folded in her wallet, where his photograph should be.

But she is fortunate, within all things. Reina is a hard worker. She knows how to save, even with all the money she sends. Last week, she interviewed with a new family on Pine Tree Drive. As big as a hotel, the house was. Reina did her best not to seem overwhelmed, to answer the questions quietly but firmly, to re-sist the urge—so long bred into her, of lowering her eyes when she spoke. Yes, ma'am, she answered in English, I am very good with children. I have my own, a little boy. And Reina said it all while looking the woman in the eyes, and she didn't even cry. With a smile, she said it, pleasantly, and she tried not to think about how if she got the job, she didn't know how on earth she would keep from getting lost in that house. But if it works out, next month she will move there to be their nanny and housekeeper. She knows it will work out—the lady was very kind. She wanted a Spanish speaker so her daughter, just two years old, can learn to speak like a native. Reina cannot believe her luck. She is so close now. They will pay her even more than she makes now. And, with no living expenses, in a year Reina will have saved enough to pay someone to bring Joaquin to her, just in time to start first grade. Little by little, things are working out for Reina X., who turns twenty-three today, her birthday.

Rosario and Magda arrive and Reina gives them each a quick peck on the cheek. Vaya con Dios, she says, and the women return the blessing, though Reina didn't mean it for them. Outside the apartment door, she crosses herself quickly before descending the stairs.

———

On Sunday, a new set of white roses appear by the front door of apartment 2B. They're joined by a votive candle of La Caridad del Cobre and a medal of Saint Christopher. The following week brings pink carnations, a copy of Martí's Versos Sencillos, *two orchids, and a slice—wrapped in plastic—of bright yellow cake.*

LANA, 2012

Her first night in apartment 2B, she showers and drops to sleep. At midnight she wakes and lies in bed enveloped in silence, a cashmere silence, sumptuous luxury. Then comes the sound of tiny feet above. Beyond the ceiling, something shuffling to life.

When she wakes again, late in the afternoon, her face is blank. Not the long corridor of light, not the polished surfaces, nor the call of the fruit seller in the street below. She is somewhere unfamiliar. She sits up in this new bed and regards the bare white dresser, the empty closet. For a long time, she stares at the shuttered window as if it were mounted on the wrong side, the room a mirror image of a more familiar home. From the street, the sound of laughter and then a distant siren. When she sets her feet on the floor, the wood groans.

She stops in the living room and holds her hands to her eyes, letting them adjust to the light. By the entrance, four suitcases bristle with tags. A door slams somewhere beyond her walls. And then the sound of someone crying. In the kitchen, she pours coffee grounds into a paper-lined cone and leans against the counter waiting for the water to boil. As soon as the smell of coffee fills the kitchen, her shoulders relax. She drinks the first cup as quickly as the heat allows, clearing the last of the sleeping pills from her head.

She rolls two of the suitcases to the second bedroom and begins to unpack. Yellow afternoon light floods the room. She stands the empty canvases against the wall, unfolds an easel and sets it on the table. One by one, she arranges the paints and then the brushes. She props a canvas on the easel and stands, staring at it for a moment. From the second suitcase, she pulls out books. Poetry, mostly, which she arranges on the shelves. And then a small silver plate engraved with the crest of the Anglo-American University in Cairo. She turns it in her hands and the reflection bounces from wall to wall like a searchlight. She begins to set it on a shelf and then reconsiders. In the kitchen, she stashes the silver plate behind the pots. On her way out, she trips on the uneven floor—a depression she didn't notice—and falls hard.

Within moments comes the pounding from the apartment beneath her. A man's voice sputters through the floorboards. *Knock it off!* he yells. *Knock it off, you selfish asshole!*

———

The leasing agent told her only that the apartment sat vacant for more than a year and that's why the owner slashed the rent. The agent used that word—*slashed*—because language is always precise, even when its speakers don't mean to be.

━━━

On the second night, she wakes again in the dark. From the street, an unfolding rumbling, like an ache in the building's foundation. When it stops, a tinny melody drifts through the apartment, *something, something, something*. She turns her head, as if trying to place the song. But in the next moment, the machine-percussion starts again. She crosses the living room in her tiptoes. Lights and crew in the street below. She opens the windows. After Cairo, the late September evening should feel almost cool against her skin, warm with life. But she grimaces; the breeze carries the scent of something putrid. Workers have blocked off a corner of the road with orange cones and caution tape. A group stands inside this makeshift pen surrounding what looks like a miniature digger with its own miniature driver, and next to it a rectangular machine—a motor?—the size of a van. It's painted a sickly shade of pink. It shudders and bangs like the end of the world. A man shouts and the machine kicks off. Below, a tangle of gray tubes sweat on the pavement, their other ends vanishing into a hole in the cut-up street. The men work by floodlights that cast bat-like shadows. She stares down into the spectacle from her second-story perch as if trying to understand what she's seeing. A sewer break? The workers don't talk to one another, and even the clubbers pass in silence, not glancing at the great soup-making operation before them. And then one of the workers shouts, ¡Está bien! and the machine trembles. The rumbling ripples out like ocean waves.

She sits in front of the window like that for a long time, she watching the midnight workers; me watching her.

═══

I was born in Sagua La Grande, birthplace of wanderers: Wifredo Lam and Esteban Montejo and me, Lenin García.

Born two weeks early—siempre un desespera'o, Mamá would say throughout my childhood. A small boy with a delicate face, un trigueño like the father I never knew. After his death, Mamá moved us to the capital, into a ruin in Jesús María, where three families, including her cousins, already lived. There, I learned to walk before I turned one. By two, when my grandparents joined us, I was running. And I've been running ever since.

Even in my nightmares, I run and run, from the dog, the monster, the miliciano with his Russian rifle. Sometimes I make it home before waking. But when I try to shut the door on the beast, the door suddenly shrinks from its frame. Or the locks don't work. Or I drop the keys.

At fifteen, my mother took me across the bay to Regla, to a curandera someone knew. The curandera was a very proper lady, very thin and self-possessed, more like a schoolteacher than my image of a curandera. She took my head in her hands and looked into my eyes. Something she saw there made her pause. She looked at my mother and then back to me. After a while she said, "The ancestors speak to you from the home of your inner life. When your inner life is spare, there is nowhere for the ghosts to sit. When you furnish your spirit, the ancestors will once again find rest in you." Mamá and I laughed at this on the ferry home. But we returned to her several times. We talked of my dreamland pursuers, about the nature of home, about all those keys. She warned me, the last time, to be wary of solitude. That I must admit I craved it, or it would engulf me. Two nights later, I dreamt the same dream. Except this time I was the monster, chasing a shadow self through the back alleys. I chased myself right up the rotting tenement stairs and onto the landing. But this self I recognized was too quick for the monster I'd become. He slipped inside and, at the last minute, shut the door in my face. I heard the bolt turn, and I woke.

But now. Now I exist in eternal wakelessness. Even my nightmares are slowly fading. I am left only with the work that must be completed: one last run before darkness closes.

———

She has been careful to avoid the neighbors, moving like someone trying to hide. But one morning someone knocks on her door. She opens, first a sliver and then the door swings wide. An old woman standing there, holding a cake.

"Good afternoon!" the old woman says. "Welcome to the Helena."

"Oh . . . Thank you."

"I'm Miriam, your next-door neighbor—here, I made this for you."

"That's so kind," she says. She hesitates a moment and then takes the cake from Miriam's hands. "I would invite you in, but . . ."

"No, no, I just wanted to say hello." But Miriam doesn't move from the threshold.

"Okay, then. Thank you again."

Miriam says something in Arabic and steps forward as if to touch her.

She steps back. "I'm sorry, I don't speak the language."

"But you came from Egypt, no?"

"Who told you that?"

"My sincere apologies if I've offended you."

"No offense, I'm just not Egyptian."

Miriam nods. "I'm Miriam. Apartment 3B, right next door. If you ever need anything . . ."

"Thank you. Thank you kindly." And then, as if reconsidering something, she says, "I appreciate your attentions, but I'm busy at the moment." She shifts the cake to her left hand and extends her right. "I'm Lana."

Miriam smiles and shakes her hand. "Lana! Like the actress."

"It wasn't her real name," Lana says. "Anyway, thank you again, and good afternoon to you."

Lana shuts the door and bolts it. She spends a moment in front of the peephole and then walks to the kitchen and throws the cake in the trash.

———

She mixes paints on the palette, dragging a spot of black into the white with a knife, kneading them together like butter. When she's satisfied, she sits in front of the easel, the canvas blank. With a wide brush, she covers the surface with a pale gray. Next, she mixes white into blue, and with another brush spreads a sky over the top half of the canvas, not waiting for the underlayer to dry. She lays down four rough strokes of ocher in the center, another stroke for what will become the neck and then the shoulders. The light shifts. She paints for most of the afternoon, forgetting to eat. When she's done, she opens the window. A mockingbird trills four bursts of song that end with a quick staccato *beep beep beep*. After a pause, it starts up again. Lana stands at the window, trying to find the source of the sound.

———

In the rooms we shared in Jesús María, a bedsheet with a faded flower pattern established the boundaries of our privacy. Each time a new cousin arrived, another bedsheet went up, yellowed with age.

I was eight or nine years old when Hurricane Georges struck. We passed the storm on the ground floor with the other families. We didn't know what was happening upstairs, but it sounded like war. After the wind died, we tried to ascend. A waterfall greeted us where the stairs used to be—it was like a kind of fairy tale. The faces of the adults were very grave and my mother kept repeating, "Dios Santo!" But for us kids, it unfolded like a fantastic adventure. When you're little, any break from the normal march of things is thrilling. The irresistible allure of chaos: Palm fronds and branches where there shouldn't be any. A river flowing past the mismatched chairs. Crabs in the sofa!

Part of the roof had collapsed, filling the upper rooms with water, but our floor was still habitable, so we returned that same night. By the next morning, under a brilliant sun, everyone got to work. The women mopped while the men set out across the city to scavenge supplies. Late that evening, my cousins joined the group laying a tarp over the hole in the roof. Someone said that the government promised to distribute cement tiles later that week and everyone laughed. We slept with one eye opened for a while, but we slept. We were together. And when you're together, everything is bearable.

———

Lana is sleeping and doesn't hear the door until the knocking wakes her.

"I'm sorry," Lana says, opening the door for Miriam. And because she is still sleepy, she is honest: "I took an extra sleeping pill last night."

Alarm flashes across Miriam's face. Lana is looking away and doesn't catch it, but I do.

It is almost noon and Miriam has brought lunch.

"You don't need to do that," Lana says. She shifts from one leg to another before finally accepting the foil-covered dish.

"Stuffed cabbage," Miriam says.

Lana uncovers the dish. "Ooof. That's strong."

Miriam looks down and Lana's eyes soften.

"I'm sorry," she says. "That wasn't very gracious of me."

"No, it wasn't."

Lana pauses and holds the dish up. "It's still warm."

Miriam smooths the front of her dress.

"You can eat it now if you want."

Lana grimaces. "Maybe in a few hours," she says. But Miriam doesn't move from the door. The women stand looking at one another for a moment before Lana finally steps aside, gesturing with her free arm. "Please come in."

Miriam pauses, sensing me near, but she enters anyway.

"I'll put this away," Lana says. "Would you like some tea? I'm sorry, all I have is green."

When Lana returns with the tea, she says, "I'm sorry I don't have any sugar or honey."

"So many apologies!" Miriam says. "Did you enjoy the sfouf?"

"I'm sorry?"

"The sfouf. The cake I brought last time."

"Oh . . . yes. It was delicious. Thank you."

"I'm very happy you enjoyed it," Miriam says. "It has always been my son's favorite cake. It's turmeric that gives it the strong yellow color."

"You're a baker?"

Miriam laughs. "Yes, I never thought of it that way, but yes, baking is a hard science. You could say I'm a baker who trained as a chemist."

"Oh, so you're a chemist?"

Miriam shakes her head. "Was. In Beirut, before the war. Now I'm just a refugee who bakes. The profession I've held the longest. And you? Are you from Miami originally?"

"No," Lana says.

Miriam waits for her to continue. But Lana only sits, sipping her tea.

"You don't have family here?" Miriam asks.

"I don't."

"Ah. Well, I am lucky that I still have my Daoud," Miriam says, and looks into her cup. "He visits me often."

"Your son?" Lana says, searching Miriam's face carefully. Miriam nods.

"He was always such a funny little boy, Daoud." But then Miriam stops, her eyes shimmering.

"The weather is turning cooler," Miriam says. "At least in the early mornings when I take my walk. You should come with me. It's a relief. Sometimes I go so early the workers are still there."

"I've seen them," Lana says. "What are they doing?"

"Trying to dig us out of our own mess."

"Sewers?"

"Flooding," Miriam says. "Every year it gets worse. When I first moved here, it rarely rained hard enough to flood the streets. But now the smallest shower and we're underwater. It doesn't even have to rain—just the full moon will do it. You've probably seen them all over the city."

"I haven't gotten out much."

"Why not?" Miriam says. "Why don't you join me on a walk tomorrow morning?"

"Thank you," Lana says and stands. "But I'm too busy."

=====

Knock it off, you stupid bitch! Lana has dropped her keys. She drops them again and again. The next morning, still dark out, she's woken by the armor-piercing shrapnel of AC/DC. The music cuts, and from below a man screams, *That's for the keys, you inconsiderate cunt!*

Lana lies in bed. When the silence returns, she hears them: the night creatures moving above her, beyond the ceiling.

=====

One year, for my birthday, my uncle in New Jersey sent me a book of dinosaurs. The faded red cover was worn at the edges: a secondhand kids' book, published in the 1970s and already outdated by the time I held it—that's the kind of gifts he sent, cast-offs, old clothes that smelled of hamburgers, tennis shoes worn unevenly at the heels. But the book, despite my uncle, became a treasure. I understood very little of the English text, but I lay on my cot for hours looking through the illustrations. The book was so old that it still presented tyrannosaurus as if it walked upright, human-like. I turned pages and just like that I passed from the Triassic to the Jurassic to the Cretaceous: 165 million years in a single afternoon, triceratops, brontosaurus, and stegosaurus all drinking from the same pond as a volcano erupts eternally in the distance. Geological time still gives me a good kind of vertigo. Sixty-five million years since the last tyrannosaurus tyrannized the first tiny mammal hiding in its burrow. And sixty-five million years for a handful of the burrowers to stay alive through molten rain, ice ages, eruptions, to persist in this struggle of days and nights, long enough to endure.

=====

A woman stops Lana as she's leaving the apartment. She wears a housedress, a bata de casa like the ones my mother used to wear. The woman grabs Lana's wrist.

"You're not afraid to be living there?"

Lana shakes free.

"Sorry?"

Bata de Casa watches Lana.

After a moment she says, "You don't know, do you?"

"Don't know what?" Lana says.

"About the apartment . . ."

"If you'll excuse me, I need to get to the store before it closes," Lana says, and starts for the stairs.

"You don't know about him, the boy who died here!"

Lana waves an arm in the air but doesn't turn around.

"Lenin! What a name!" the woman shouts after Lana. "What idiot kind of mother gives her innocent little baby a name like Lenin? Can you think of anything stupider? But what can you expect from these people? That generation is ruined, ruined. I read in a book how damaged they all are . . . zombies, the writer called them, and that is exactly what they are. All of them. They have spent the last fifty years scamming and scrambling. They don't respect anything. How could they? A lifetime of the government lying to you, your neighbor lying to you. Your own mother . . . Lenin! . . . lying to you. What is there left to believe in? The walking dead is what they are. They've stopped thinking. Parasites! These are the kind of people who shouted, *Gusanos*, at us. People who could not wait to get their hands on our property."

The downstairs door slams shut, but Bata de Casa keeps yelling. She turns to the closed door and shouts into the apartment. "Do you know what kind of people became Communists? The lazy, the stupid, the petty criminal. The envious!"

That terrible summer, when everyone we knew was leaving and even the stray cats had vanished from the streets, Mamá cut up a new floor rag, marinated it in mojo overnight, breaded it, and fried it up like bistec to sell in the streets. The baby downstairs never stopped crying. I've never told anyone this. From that time, I carry only impressions, the half-realized world of the child: the bistec that you had to chew and chew until it finally broke apart, never quite dissolving; the watery milk; the lines of people everywhere; the darkened buildings I accompanied my mother to, in and out of crumbling rooms, a handful of chicharos here, a small bag of wormy rice there, now and then a few grams of minced meat that my mother never tasted, kept from her own family—all of it going to me. We walked and walked, all over Havana, and Mamá grew so thin she seemed like a ghost beneath the loose dresses she wore throughout that summer.

All that waiting, for the buses that never came, for the day's single meal, for the electricity to return. Walking next to my mother, I developed a game: si solo. I played it when my stomach grumbled, while we waited under the sun beneath a boarded window where someone might appear with something to sell, I played it at night, when I lay next to my mother, listening to both our bellies complain. I played it in our hungry walks around the city. I played it on those rare days when my mother persuaded someone to watch me and I found myself in a stranger's damp room, trying to tune out the yelling. Si solo. Si solo tuviéramos agua, si solo un pedacito de pan con mantequilla, si solo hubiera nacido un príncipe en el reino de las maravillas. I can speak English well now, but I still prefer the Spanish. *Si solo* sounds truer than *If only*. One rhymes with loneliness. The other just means empty hope. *Si solo Papá no hubiera muerto.* In Spanish, the phrase contains the isolation that my father carried back from Angola.

Until I was thirteen, I believed my father died a hero in Africa, fighting for the continent's liberation. And then one afternoon, the special period behind us, life growing easier, I returned early from school and overheard my grandfather shouting at my mother. I hid until he left the building. That evening, shut behind our curtain, I whispered, Is it true that Papá killed himself? My mother looked up suddenly and understood. She tried to take me in her arms, but I pushed her away. Just tell me the truth, I said. So she did.

One night, when Lana returns to the apartment close to midnight, her eyes go to the couch. Something looks wrong. All the pillows have been moved to one side. She listens. The apartment is still and quiet. She checks the closet, the bathroom. Slowly, she opens the door to the second bedroom. One of her canvases lies facedown. Mice. She sees the proof of their intrusion: there and there and there are the droppings. She checks the locks. In her bedroom, everything is as it should be. She showers, takes her pills, and slips into bed. Her dreams—do they fill with raindrops? The steady drizzle of the mice tap-tapping on the ceiling.

"Some nights I hear you crying." Miriam has come by with almond cookies.

Lana squints. "It's not me," she says. "It comes from another apartment somewhere, maybe next door, through the walls."

Miriam touches her arm and Lana pulls back.

That afternoon instead of painting, she vacuums. The repetitive back-and-forth seems to soothe her. As she's putting the machine away, there's a hard knock at the door.

"Miami Beach police."

Lana looks through the peephole.

She opens the door. A short fat man in a mustache. A tall one with a hand on his gun.

"Good afternoon, ma'am," says the fat one.

"Can I help you?"

"One of your neighbors has filed a noise nuisance complaint," he says.

"Noise?" Lana says. "It's three in the afternoon."

"Mind if we come in?" The tall one already has his foot inside.

Lana steps away from the door. "Someone actually complained about the noise?"

"Reports of shouting and heavy machinery."

Now both cops are inside.

The tall one is looking around. "Why don't you put down some rugs in here?"

"Are you serious?"

"We have reason to believe you're harassing your neighbor downstairs."

"That's nonsense. He's harassing me! I have to be able to move around my own apartment."

"We were down there just now," the fat one says. "You had some kind of machinery going on."

Lana points to the vacuum cleaner.

The tall one touches his gun again. He's standing now in the hallway, looking left to right from one bedroom to the other. His eyes move from Lana's bed, still unmade, and back to her. He returns his hand to the gun.

"The complaint says that at night the resident can hear you with your boyfriend."

"I live alone here. What are you talking about!"

"Loud sex. I believe that's the wording in the complaint."

"What?"

She takes a few steps back to the door and opens it.

"I'd like your badge numbers, please," she manages to say.

The cops laugh. They, too, must notice the shaking in her knees. The tall one stands very close to Lana. He points to the numbers on his badge. "There you go, honey, got that?"

They pause long enough to let her know they could stay if they wanted. They're doing her a favor; she should be grateful. Tall cop starts to step across the threshold, but then he stops, again, inches from Lana's face.

"Try to keep it down, okay, miss?"

When they leave, she double-bolts the door.

———

Lana sits before the easel. She blocks off the background with dabs of green and beige. Near the bottom, the jagged outline of palms. Then she returns to the face, dark brown underlayer for the hair. Thick brows beneath the hairline, the rough oval of eyes, a darker beige where the nose will go. A shadow beneath the chin.

"They were just like the security at the Cairo airport," Lana says. "One mean one, one quiet one. Fascists resemble one another more than brothers."

The light through the window dims and she turns on the overhead lights. Flicks on another long-armed lamp clamped to the desk. She paints through the dinner hour. Brushstroke by brushstroke, the face comes into focus. She stops very late.

In her bedroom, Lana drops her clothes in a pile and slips into her white nightgown. She takes two pills and falls asleep almost instantly. Within moments, the walls contract and the shiver resonates like cracking in the beams. The wood floor braces itself against the load. The air conditioner cycles off, and now comes the complaint of old pipes, the piano music that begins and stops and begins again, the tapping of thin branches on the windows. From beyond, the muffled voices that sometimes sound like sobbing. Lana wakes. She lies in the dark, listening. Her eyes are opened wide in terror, but her limbs are rigid, paralyzed.

───

Morning steals across the bare floor of apartment 2B; light slithers into the corners. The wood cracks. From the bedroom, Lana emerges in bare feet, small quiet steps to the bathroom, where the sound of vomiting is punctuated by the flush of the toilet. After a while, she enters the living room, where the light has already shifted. She sits at the dining room table and puts her head in her hands.

───

It took almost a year, but the cement tiles materialized. Soon after we patched the hole in the roof, though, the building plunged into mourning. A late afternoon in August. Another downpour had soaked the city for a week, and finally the sun returned. The children were playing outside, under the shade of the balconies. I was on our floor and heard it. The roof's collapsed again, I thought. But the screaming came from the street. By the time I made it down the crumbling stairs, such a crowd had gathered that I couldn't see it. Thank god I couldn't see it. The men who had tried to rescue her didn't sleep for two nights and there was such a wail of lamentation up and down Jesús María that for a moment I believed the government itself would collapse. Such was the rage in the street. María Elena del Carmen, six years old. Jumping rope directly beneath the second-floor balcony. There was no saving her. That night, very late, my mother crept into my cot and held me and held me.

=====

A knock on her door, which Lana ignores. Then another one. And another. Lana looks through the peephole, and sighs. She opens the door.

"¡Oye! Ya me iba marchar," the young woman says. "Toma." She pushes a dish into Lana's hands.

"Sorry. Don't speak the language."

"A welcome flan. Not to be confused with a welcome plan."

"This is very kind . . ."

"Yolanda Sanchez," the woman says and holds out her hand. "I'm your neighbor, 4B, next to Miriam. She told me all about you."

"Oh, that's surprising," Lana says. "There isn't much to tell."

Yolanda laughs. "Exactly! So I said to myself, I'll go look in on the mysterious Lana myself."

Lana shifts in place. "I'd invite you in . . ."

Yolanda pushes past her. "Thank you, but I can only stay a moment!"

She looks around the apartment and then at Lana.

"I like what you've done. Spare, but clean."

"I'm sorry?"

"I meant to come by earlier," Yolanda says. "To say hello, but I was traveling."

"Oh?"

"To Cuba," Yolanda says. "On business. You ever been?"

"Why would I?"

"You're not Cuban?"

"No."

"Oh, right. Miriam said something about Cairo."

"I'm not Egyptian, either."

"Okeydokey! Woman doesn't want to talk too much, I get it," Yolanda says.

Lana stares at her.

"Thank you, don't mind if I take a chair, or as we say in Cuban, drink a chair." Yolanda spreads her arms wide. "Cuban born and raised, but six years in Miami. In this building it will be three years in February. It's not the best, as you probably know, but it's a palace compared to where I came from."

"Is there a mice infestation or something?"

Yolanda bursts out laughing. "Generations of them! More like a mouse metropolis. About once a year, maintenance lays traps in the crawl space and then it's quiet for a while, but the mice always return. I think they're just getting smarter and smarter up there. We're inadvertently breeding a class of Einstein mice."

"No one told me anything about that," Lana says.

"Nah, why would they?" Yolanda laughs.

"But they're a health hazard."

"Are they?" Yolanda shrugs. "Never bothered me."

Lana is still standing. She shifts in place, looks at the door.

"Sit, sit," Yolanda says, as if this were her apartment.

"It's just that I'm in the middle of something right now."

"Oh, it can wait, mujer!" Yolanda says. "Listen, I came by because I heard Fefa in the hallway ranting the other day."

"Fefa?"

"'*They don't belong here,*' that Fefa, crazy Fefa, '*sombies, blah blah.*' Siempre el mismo tema," Yolanda says. "Don't pay her any mind."

"She said something about a boy dying here. In this apartment."

Yolanda's expression doesn't change, but for a moment she looks away.

Lana sits down. "Okay, is there something I should know about?"

═══

¡Tienes que llevar al niño a alguien o va' terminar como tu marido. No comas mierda, Marisol!

I was too big already, but my mother invited me to sit on her lap. She rocked us for a while, me growing sleepy against her bony chest. I can still smell her, the fried onions and sour scent of work that hung about her always and that, because it was hers, filled me with peace. My mother wove her fingers into my curls, now and then pulling them, stretching my scalp up and out—a feeling of complete transport. We rocked like that in silence, the last moments of my innocence. When she finally spoke, it was without clearing her throat, or calling me by name, the way she usually did. I was old enough, she said. I should know the story before I heard it from someone else, someone with evil intention.

My father finished three tours in Angola. They conceived me after the first. But after my father returned from the second, he refused to even kiss my mother. Her family noticed how he'd grown thin, his skin—always so warm and deep—now ashen. His clothes hung from him. He never talked about what he saw, what happened over there. He returned to Sagua for the last time in June of 1991, eyes already like a tomb. I was a baby, de brazos, as we say, naked against the heat of that summer. Mamá was afraid to leave me with my father and instead strapped me to herself to stand in the lines that seemed to grow longer and longer each passing day. Colas for la libreta, colas for the milk that I was still eligible for, colas that wound like a serpent around the ruins. Colas at the clinic, where no one could diagnose her husband's strange illness. An orderly who was probably in her early twenties told them hearing loss was common among the Angola veterans. The lump that developed under his ear probably a parasite. Within months, sores covered his thin chest. As the weather turned cooler, he took to wrapping himself in a blanket on the front porch of their hut, shivering, talking nonsense between labored breaths. By Three Kings Day, he was unable to even speak for the rattle in his lungs. My mother begged her brother in New Jersey to send antibiotics, which finally arrived in April. But the pneumonia persisted.

"It's true what you heard Abuelo say," my mother told me as dusk fell around us and the call of roosting birds sounded a choir up and down our darkening street. "But your father didn't want to be a burden. He didn't give up. He was a good and brave veteran who finally broke under his troubles."

I couldn't ask her about the other thing my grandfather called him. I was more afraid of that word—and my own shameful desires—than I was of death.

===

The next time Miriam knocks, Lana doesn't even look through the peephole.

"Come in," she says.

Miriam hands her a plate of cookies. "Mahmoul."

"Listen. Why are all of you being so solicitous of me?"

"I don't know this word, *solicitous*."

"All of you so friendly, bringing food, dropping in—it's like a 1950s Welcome Wagon," Lana says. "Does it have anything to do with the boy who committed suicide?"

Miriam crosses herself.

"Yolanda told me the whole story."

"Why would she do that?" Miriam says. "You need to

regain your strength, you don't need to worry about what happened here."

"How would you know if I needed to regain my strength? You don't know anything about me."

Miriam stares at her. "Please, habibti, let's sit."

This time Lana doesn't protest that she doesn't understand. She looks at Miriam evenly. When she's taken a chair across from her, Lana says, "Look, I came to Miami Beach precisely because I don't know anyone here. I don't need mothers."

"Everyone needs a mother," Miriam says quietly.

Lana looks away.

"Do you all feel guilty? Is that it?"

"Guilty?" Miriam considers this. "This word is for crimes. Not guilty. But sorry, maybe. For ignoring him."

"Shit," Lana says.

"That's not why we come by," Miriam says. "Not really . . . I don't know. In my case, I was thinking more of my own son. How I couldn't save him. How we can't save any of them."

Lana leans forward, locking eyes with Miriam. "What do you mean? You said your son visits you."

"My son, yes," Miriam says. She cannot hold Lana's stare and looks away. "He visits me, though it's been more than forty years."

Miriam lifts her face to the ceiling.

"He would be an old man now," Miriam says. She returns Lana's gaze, steady. "And yet every day the boy visits me, the boy I lost."

Lana hesitates. "In the war?"

Miriam nods.

"I think back now, and it is all like a dream, a terrible dream," she says after a moment. She interlaces her fingers as if in prayer. The ruby on her left hand catches the light.

"How did we survive it all? My building was three blocks from the Green Line. Two of the north-facing windows had blown out, and I'd cut up a shower curtain to cover them. The plastic expanded and contracted in the wind, like lungs. But you couldn't stay indoors forever. You had to go out for water, for food. I was a woman, all alone. Those of us left in the building, we helped one another, warily, protecting the little bit that we had, but helping . . . sharing, when we could. That's the only reason I survived. There were times of the day when the snipers were worse. You didn't go out then. In my neighborhood, they were most active in the mornings, when the children were supposed to be going to school . . . and in the afternoon."

Miriam stops. Lana is quiet. After a while, Miriam continues. "Did you know that human beings can be like this? Normal human beings, the boys that you took care of, the friends of your son, nice boys. Did you know this could happen? That some terrible blood would rise in them and set them on rooftops like dark angels, deciding who would live and who would die? After war, it is so hard to believe . . . so hard."

"I know . . ." Lana begins to reach for Miriam's hand, then stops.

"You went out at dusk," Miriam continues. "Thinking that's when their aim wouldn't be as good. And you scurried like a rat, hugging the ruins, keeping your back to the pockmarked concrete. Skittering back and forth across the city like this, like the lowest animal, just to buy a bit of bread, a small bag of alhams. And when an old man was shot just behind you, you kept running, you did not turn around, you ran past the ruins and you did not stop. You never turned around; you understand?"

She begins to cry. And Lana finally reaches across the cookies and puts her hand on Miriam's. I watch first Lana's shoulders relax, and then Miriam's.

"Who really knows what happens when we die?" Miriam says. "What do we know of this world and its ten thousand forms? Every day, Daoud visits with me. Every day, he and I save that nest of serins again, the nest that fell to the pavement on a cold blue spring day before the war, when Daoud was still the little boy who took our hands, between me and his father, still alive, then, both still alive."

She turns to Lana with cloudy eyes.

"Birth and death are perched on a precipice, my dear one. The years in between, we cling to love."

―――

That night, Lana searches for me. In the closets, the cupboards. I walk behind her. She searches for me in the living room, scans the armchair beneath the window, the shelves. I walk behind her. She turns over the paintings hanging on the wall: a beach wilderness; a moonlit ocean; a print of a grand, colonnaded plaza, lines architecturally precise. All of them devoid of people. The dining room table with its four wooden chairs. Even the fruit bowl of smoky glass. None of it is hers. A furnished apartment waits for ghosts. She paces the rooms in her socks, treading as softly as she can. I walk behind her. She stops at the depression in the kitchen floor and bends down to touch it. At the bedroom door she pauses at the threshold. She has never noticed the painted lump stuck to the frame. She returns with a butter knife and loosens the gummy paint until the mezuzah comes away from the frame. She catches it just before it falls.

It was the fastest way to obtain hard currency after the special period. The summer I turned sixteen. Yoni told me about it. He and I met behind one of the niches in the Colon Cemetery. Yoni brought one of the foreign magazines, as always. Men and women doing all sorts of things to one another. The women flaunted enormous breasts, but it was the bodies of the men that stirred me, a desire that seemed to come from my belly button. The first time I felt it, I confused it with an urge to urinate. "It has never occurred to me to be ashamed," Yoni told me when I confessed. "It's just something I need to do, like breathing. Don't be so afraid of pleasure, querido."

When we were done, Yoni smiled. "You are getting pretty good."

He reached into his front pocket and drew out what looked like a baseball made of dollars. Dollars, hundreds of them. I must have opened my eyes wide—a new kind of desire, which made Yoni laugh.

"You go down to the Yara in those shorts you're wearing," Yoni said. "I'll introduce you to some of my friends. It's easy. Some of the men come in thirty seconds. You only have to show them your dick. That gets you a few dollars, especially if it's already hard. Pleasure, my friend. That's the real currency! Pleasure. Stop being such a dour communist and enjoy yourself."

THAT FIRST WEEKEND, I MADE THIRTY DOLLARS, American ones, more money than I ever held in my hands at once. My first impulse was to give it all to Mamá. But she was no fool, that daughter of las Canarias. She would know. So I kept the money, a signing bonus. That Sunday night, I told Mamá I found a job tending the pool at El Nacional— she wouldn't be allowed into the hotel anyway, so how would she find out? Just a few hours a day after school, I promised. The Italians, I said, tipped especially well. And the hotel gave its workers the food that was left over at the end of the day. Mamá praised God and, to my surprise, began to cry.

"Ya, ya, Mamita. This is our lucky time now!"

That's what I said, and I believed it.

She's cleaning her brushes over the bathroom sink when someone knocks on the door. Lana stands for a moment. The loneliness that has hardened her face all morning melts a little bit. She dries her hands.

When she opens the door, it's Yolanda, shaking a yellow pouch in her hands. "Are you up for a game?"

"What is that? Dominoes?"

"Bananagrams," Yolanda says. "It's like dominoes for literate people. My first English teacher in Miami taught us to play, and I got hooked."

"I was just finishing up something."

"Painting?" Yolanda says.

Lana's face darkens.

"Don't worry, mujer! I'm not spying on you. Just look at your hands—they're covered in paint."

"Yes, I was finishing up a painting."

"So you're a painter!"

"No, no. It started as a way to notice things and now it's how I remember them," Lana says. "Just a hobby."

Yolanda shakes the yellow bag.

"So is this!" Without waiting for Lana to protest, Yolanda takes a chair at the dining room table. She unzips the pack and the tiles scatter.

"It's very easy," Yolanda says. "You can even play on your own."

She turns the tiles over and starts to mix them.

Yolanda counts out the tiles in Spanish and turns them over.

"Carajo, both *x*'s" she says. "Sit. Take twenty-one tiles and just try to form some words. When you've used up all the letters, you say, 'Peel,' and then we both grab another one. If you don't like what you get, like these stupid *x*'s, you can dump and get three more."

"Not dominoes," Lana says. "More like Scrabble for the deranged."

Yolanda laughs. She's shifting her tiles back and forth and says, "Sit, sit!"

Lana pauses a moment. And then she pulls out a chair.

"I haven't been able to stop thinking about the man you told me about."

"Lenin?"

"Fefa was all worked up about the name."

"Of course she was!" Yolanda says. "I'm guessing it only became popular in Cuba after Fefa left. Growing up, I knew three Lenins. For a time, I even went with a Lenin."

"It's a real name?"

"In Cuba it is. The Cuban Lenins are more real than the real Lenin, whose real name wasn't even Lenin at all. But everyone in Miami is a historical illiterate. If you mentioned a dude named *Vlad Ulyanov*, they won't know who you're talking about."

"Lenin," Lana says. "Why was he unhappy?"

Yolanda looks up from her tiles.

"Why did he do it, do you think?" Lana says.

"What does it matter, the why?" Yolanda says. "*Why did my husband leave me? Why did I get fired? Why were they arrested?*" Yolanda returns to her word grid. "When my father died of lung cancer the first thing people said was, *Lo siento,* and the second thing was, *Did he smoke?* Because, of course, if there's a reason, then it won't happen to us, right?"

Lana lowers her eyes. "I just think that maybe he didn't want to die. Just rest."

"Oh please, mujer," Yolanda says. "Don't you go and romanticize it. That's a virus you can catch just by thinking about it. I'm serious. That's how Cuba ended up with the highest suicide rate in Latin America. Mujer, are you listening?"

——

She has the windows open. Sounds drift up from the street: someone whistling in the alley, wind in the coconut palm, the sound of a motorcycle tearing off on a distant street, the mockingbird with its strange trill. She reads for half an hour and is asleep within minutes of turning off the bedside lamp.

She sleeps soundlessly, trance just this side of waking. But sometime in the night her limbs go rigid. And then a faint cry from her throat, like a strangled scream.

——

In the morning, she lies in bed, looking up at the ceiling. She dresses slowly, makes her coffee. She makes a second cup and then a third, the sleeping pills harder and harder to clear.

She washes the cup, turns it over in the drainer, and returns to the dining room table, where last night she left the paint-encrusted mezuzah. She takes it in her hands, turns it over, and removes the pins that held it to the wall.

She puts down a layer of paper towels and fetches a small brush and bottle of paint thinner. Slowly, she works to dissolve the layers of paint: white, pink, pale green. She is cleaning the pins when someone knocks on the door.

"Jesus Christ," she mumbles. "Ridiculous."

Whoever it is goes away.

When the last of the paint is gone, Lana opens the compartment and unrolls the prayer. It's intact, untouched by the years. She stares at it for a moment, rolls it back up, and tucks it back into the holder.

Late that afternoon, she returns with a paper bag from Ace to find Miriam waiting for her outside her apartment.

"Is everything okay?"

"Yes," Lana says.

"I came by earlier," Miriam says. "There's a friend I'd like you to meet."

"I don't date." Lana turns the keys in her lock, but doesn't invite Miriam in.

"My dear one, why would I add to your troubles?" Miriam says. "The friend I'd like you to meet is a very old woman, and she needs some help.

"I don't have time right now," Lana says. She steps across the threshold, doorknob in her hands.

"I just want to introduce the two of you. Her name is Milagros. She lives downstairs." Miriam drops her voice and points to the ground. "Next to you-know-who."

Lana makes a face.

"She has a woman who takes care of her, cooks and cleans,

but she needs someone to read to her," Miriam says. "She's blind in one eye."

"Why me?" Lana leans against the doorframe.

Miriam pulls her head back. "She asked me for someone who can read English well and I thought of you . . ."

Miriam searches Lana's face.

"I'm sorry, but I don't have time for that," Lana says.

"She told me she's willing to pay you."

"Oh my god, no!" Lana says. "I don't need money . . . This is the woman with the walker? White hair and blue eyes?"

Miriam smiles. "Maybe it's true what they say about you."

"Who's 'they'? And what do 'they' say about me?"

"That you're a spy."

"What nonsense people speak! I just notice stuff!"

"Well, what you've noticed is true," Miriam says. "She's lived here forever, even before me. I met her a few days after she was attacked."

"Attacked?" Lana says.

"After 9/11. Someone threw a stone through her window," Miriam says. She has lowered her voice to a whisper. "Milagros was sitting by the window reading, and because fate is cruel, the glass shattered over her face and ruined her right eye."

"Doesn't seem like that kind of neighborhood."

Miriam closes her eyes and shakes her head. "She was attacked because of her last name, Alcalá. Those months after 9/11 were not easy for many of us."

"A hate crime?" Lana says. "Did she report it?"

"Her aide did, against Milagros's wishes. I had just moved here—what a welcome! The police came by my apartment the next morning asking if I'd heard anything."

"Had you?"

"Nothing," Miriam says. "As I recall, there was a storm that night. Maybe I heard shouting. Imagine my horror when I learned some racists threw a stone through Milagros's window."

"Because of her last name?"

Miriam nods.

"I don't know," Lana says, her hand still on the door. "That sounds like a big assumption."

"They shouted something bad. I also thought that she was Arab, so I went down to comfort her. Imagine how funny to learn that she's Spanish all the way back, which of course doesn't mean she's not Arab!" Miriam laughs. "Milagros is a descendant of a former president of Spain or something like that—I can't remember his name now. He fought the fascists."

"What a story," Lana says.

"A huge rock right through the front window," Miriam says. "The police spent three days knocking on all the neighbors' doors and harassing everyone and, of course, they never solved the crime."

"Doesn't surprise me," Lana says.

"So will you come?"

"Not right now," Lana says. "I'm sorry."

Lana lines up the holes and gently hammers the mezuzah back to the frame. She stands in front of it for a while and then reaches out her hand to touch it.

⸻

Later that week, Miriam is waiting for Lana at the entrance to the building.

"Please, habibti, come with me," she says.

Lana lifts her grocery bags. "I don't have time right now."

"It will just be a moment."

An apartment door opens and a woman in a walker shouts out, "Oye!" The voice strong and deep in the frail body.

Miriam kisses her on both cheeks. The woman turns, holding out her hand.

"Welcome, you must be Lana," she says. "I'm Milagros, though I've never managed any."

"Sorry. Don't speak the language," Lana says.

Milagros looks at Miriam: "You said she was Cuban?"

"I did not, you imagined that."

Lana holds up her bags. "I'm sorry, but I can't visit today."

"Nonsense," Milagros says. "It will just be a minute. Candelaria can stash your things in the fridge."

"I'm sorry, but—" Lana stops as Miriam takes her free hand.

Milagros smiles. "Give an old woman the pleasure of extending some hospitality," she says.

Inside, Miriam moves to help her friend into a chair, but Milagros pushes her away.

"You sit!" she commands. "I can manage on my own just fine."

Milagros's apartment betrays none of the trappings of her age or class. The couch's straight lines signal a spare, almost austere modernism that is tempered by a round wooden table, neatly piled with books and a trio of orchids. The only photo on the side table is a black-and-white of a strikingly beautiful woman.

Lana takes a seat on the couch. When Milagros seems satisfied that Miriam is not planning to leap to her aid, she lowers herself slowly. At the last moment, she lets go of the walker and drops suddenly into the armchair.

"Candelaria!" she shouts. "El café!"

A few moments later, a middle-aged woman appears with a silver tray.

"Candelaria is a spy in my daughter's employ," Milagros tells Lana.

"Ay, Señora Alcalá, no sea tan mala," the woman says, smiling. She sets the tray down with its three demitasse cups and a saucer of sugar. Lana and Miriam take their coffee black, but Milagros pours three spoonfuls of sugar into her own tiny cup.

"¡Ay, Señora, así no!" Candelaria cries. "The sugar was for your guests!"

"You see what I mean?" Milagros says. Then, turning to Candelaria, "Don't tell Carmencita, okay? It will only worry her."

Milagros winks at them. "At my age, what does it matter?

I'd rather have a last sweet sip of coffee than worry about losing my toes."

Candelaria shakes her head and is about to pick up the tray when Milagros stops her.

"Querida, take these bags to the kitchen, please," Milagros says.

"Oh no, no need," Lana says. "There's nothing that needs to be refrigerated."

Candelaria nods and retreats with the tray.

"Not precisely in my daughter's employ," Milagros says when Candelaria has left. "Medicare pays most of her wages. And my daughter is fine with that, even though she's married to an attack-dog Republican and they both worship like peasants at the altar of Fox News."

She cackles happily and closes her eyes to sip the last syrupy dregs in her cup.

She sets the cup down and looks at Lana.

"So you're Lana, then. Miriam said you might do me the favor of your company now and then."

Lana looks at Miriam and then back to the old woman.

"You see," Lana begins, "I don't have a lot of time, and—"

"Time!" Milagros says. "None of us have time! I saw you looking at the photo. I was beautiful, wasn't I?"

Milagros smiles at the woman in the photo, and returns to Lana.

"Don't look so surprised!" She laughs. "Don't you know that old age is like night in the tropics? It falls suddenly! You'll see: one moment, the red sky is alive with roosting birds. And the next, you cannot make out your own arms across your chest."

======

The mice grow more and more bold. All night, they scurry back and forth in a frenzy above Lana's head. Lana calls the agent and leaves a message. She waits a week and calls again and leaves another.

Finally, she gets a phone call from the building manager.

Later that afternoon, when Yolanda drops by, Lana tells her, "Armando says they're going to call an exterminator for the building."

"Of course! They'll set some traps and the mice will have a nice little feast," Yolanda says.

She shakes the yellow bag. "Up for a game?" She doesn't wait for Lana to answer.

"So an exterminator, huh?" she says when she sits down. Within moments, she's started a crossword: s*word*, *dirt*, *sight*.

"That's what Armando said."

"Yeah, well, mice are nothing, let me tell you," Yolanda says. "On Beales, we had rats. Big toothy fellows. Here, you might find them on a leash. In Cuba, they just terrorized everyone."

She picks through her tiles.

"Not a single *e*! One summer, one of them finally bit a child as he slept in his bed. So it became a problem. One of the tenants—a skinny crazy dude called Fidel, not that Fidel— offered to eliminate them. Fidel spread Borax everywhere.

The rats, they ate that shit up like candy and only grew more aggressive."

The puzzle grows words as Yolanda talks: *north, slay.*

"This went on until someone called in an espiritista." Yolanda looks up from her puzzle. "A very big woman who somehow managed to bend her immense body to the floorboards to talk softly to the rats, asking them kindly to find another place to live, preferably in the trees and underbrush, the way they had once done before humans invaded their wilderness."

Yolanda returns to her letters, rearranging words. Not looking up, she says, "Of course, the rats laughed at this. They persisted in their disorder, surprising people in the middle of the day with their confidence. So someone thought to call up Juana la Loca."

"Juana la Loca?" Lana says, still standing, as if she were waiting for Yolanda to leave. "That was her real name?"

"Not the Loca part, of course, but her real name was Juana, so maybe she felt she needed to live up to it," Yolanda says. "No one quite knew where she lived, but she usually came by once a day, at lunch, to beg for her meal. As far as I can tell they called her Loca because she refused meat. Not that anyone in those years had any meat to give away, but you know, it made them feel superior to pretend to eat it. People would give her a few handfuls of beans, some grains of rice. And in return, she promised to put in a word for them with the animals."

"With the animals?"

"She believed that the animals were divine and most of us were just devils in their way. I think she thought of humans as part of some ancient curse on the natural world. There were only a few among us who were righteous, and those, the animals protected."

"Okay."

Yolanda nods. "Definitely totally chifla'a," she says. "But she was the only one who was able to rid us of the rats."

"How?"

"It was very clever. I'll tell you. Come, sit, play a game with me already. It will clear your mind."

Yolanda breaks up her puzzle, flips all the tiles facedown and shuffles them again with both hands.

Lana finally sits across from her and selects some tiles.

"Just form words as they come to you," Yolanda says. "You can change it around as you wish, there are no rules, only that the words must make sense and not be proper names."

They sit in silence for a while, shuffling their miniature dominoes. They take their pieces and after a long while, Lana puts down *migrated* and then a few plays later, *dystopia*. Yolanda laughs.

"You'll never win being all fancy," she says. "Simple three- and four-letter words, that's how you win."

"I overcomplicate things," Lana says.

Yolanda adds *said* to her grid and looks up.

"It's okay," Yolanda says, her voice suddenly soft. "We all do." She seems to want to say something else, but then stops.

She smiles at Lana, who, for the first time, returns the smallest of smiles before shaking her head.

"So the rats," Lana says.

"The rats. Well, first, Juana did a dance while smoking a cigar. But I think this part was just a way to scam a cigar from Jorge. Then she lay facedown on the ground, flat like the dead, whispering."

"Whispering to whom?"

"*To whom*, ha-ha," Yolanda says. "You're funny. To the rats!"

"What did she say?"

"Who knows—no one could make it out . . . Anyway, then she got up and asked for some turrón. You can imagine what a joke that was during the special period. I was eight years old and I had never tasted turrón."

"What's turrón?"

"Mujer, you live in Miami and don't know turrón?"

"I'm not from here."

"It's like a nougat. I'll bring you some. Even during the special period people knew of turrón. I'll be damned but one of those motherfuckers in the building had been hoarding some alicante and managed to produce a few shards, most of which Juana la Loca ate immediately, crunching away with the three teeth left in her mouth!"

She looks over her word grid, shuffles her vowels.

"We all thought, Well, we've been had!" Yolanda says. "But no, two or three days later, Juana la Loca shows up with some traps she made from branches and wood scraps and who knows what else."

"I thought she didn't believe in killing animals."

"These weren't killing traps. They were trap-traps, with a door that shut behind the animal when it went inside. She'd loaded the doors with springs from old ballpoint pens."

"Ingenious," Lana says.

"Just Cuban!"

"Anyway, she lay them around the building with the few slivers of turrón that managed to escape her jaws. She lay a whole line of them by the front door, as if she were waiting for the rats to walk in that way, like gente fina . . . We all laughed at her. Then early one morning, as I was leaving for school, I find Juana sprawled out before the traps. Every one holds a nice plump rat. And through the slats of each trap, Juana la Loca is pushing a fresh piece of lettuce."

"I asked what she was going to do with them and she said, 'Very simple, someone is going to drive me and my charges to Miramar tonight. And I'll release them there.'"

Yolanda laughs. "No doubt the Juana la Locas of Miramar would one day bait their traps and transport the rats back to us," she says.

Lana nods, and then she's quiet for a while. She sets down tile after tile, forming words. Finally, she has used up all her tiles and calls, "Peel." They both take another tile and continue the game.

"I've lived in so many places," Lana says, as if her mind were elsewhere. "In Turkey and Albania, Sri Lanka . . ."

"What were you doing there?" Yolanda says.

Lana's eyes are unfocused, as if she's entered a trance.

"What kind of work do you do?" Yolanda asks after a moment.

"Used to do," Lana says. "I wore furrows in the earth. It seemed grand at the time."

＝＝＝

When the delivery rings for her, Lana leaps from her chair. It's the humane traps that Yolanda ordered, four of them. *Motel Mouse* say the boxes, illustrated with a little green mouse in a top hat, bag slung across its chest. Inside: a molded plastic cylinder with breathing holes on one end and a trapdoor on the other. That evening, Lana lays them out in the kitchen, baiting them with small pieces of whole-wheat bread.

The next morning the traps are all empty, the bread covered in ants.

＝＝＝

The portrait's lines are growing sharp beneath Lana's hand. Day by day, a handsome face emerges: the brows darken, the jaw sharpens. Lana paints all morning, stopping just after noon. She prepares a quick lunch and stumbles again on the uneven floor of the kitchen. Before the ghoul downstairs can hit the ceiling, she stomps hard on the floor. She jumps and jumps, rattling the glasses on the shelves. Within moments, the scream of AC/DC.

Lana clenches her fists. "That is it!" she shouts. She flies down the stairs as if possessed and pounds on the man's door.

"What is wrong with you!" she shouts into the apartment.

The music blares even louder. With both fists, she attacks the door.

"What the fuck is wrong with you!"

Lana stops at the touch of hands on her shoulders. It's Candelaria. Milagros's aide shakes her head, twirls her finger around her ear. *Loco*, she mouths.

Milagros is standing at her threshold, beckoning.

"Ven, ven!"

Lana follows Candelaria into the apartment.

"Veteran," Milagros says once the door closes.

"What?"

"Iraq," Milagros says, shouting now to be heard over the music. She looks to Candelaria, who vanishes into the kitchen. When she returns with the coffee, the music shuts off. Milagros takes a sharp breath.

"What the hell?" Lana says.

Milagros shrugs. "Man is sensitive to noise."

"Unless he's the one making it."

"We've all had to get used to him," Milagros says.

"There's no one to complain to?"

"We've tried," Milagros says. "He's friends with all the cops."

"And," says Candelaria, "he's on the condo board."

"She's right!" Milagros says. "The condo board. That pack

of degenerates. Do you know they're trying to make me get rid of the little garden I started out back?"

Lana takes a deep breath and closes her eyes.

"Condo boards are like the Politburo," Milagros says. "They're supposed to be working for you. But who is 'you'? They're working for themselves. That's the essence of communism—exactly like condo boards. They start out with good intentions: Let's form a cooperative that will look after our people's interests. And then it becomes: We must protect the board's interest. And then, by the time all the criminals join, it ends with: We have to protect ourselves."

Lana sets her little cup down. "I don't know how you can live like this. It's unbearable."

Milagros laughs. "I've lived here since before the building went condo. I've seen them come and I've seen them go."

Lana looks up suddenly. "Did you know him, the young man who—"

"I didn't," Milagros says quickly. She purses her lips. "He kept to himself. Never said hi to anyone. But I can tell you that our veteran friend here made his life a yogurt."

"I can imagine," Lana says.

"Before this you lived in Cairo, yes?"

Lana looks startled.

"Briefly, yes," she says finally.

"Did you get to visit the pyramids?"

Lana waits a long time before answering. "I did."

Milagros looks at her, waiting for her to continue.

"I saw them first at night," Lana says finally. "With . . . a colleague from the university."

Milagros raises an eyebrow.

"There's a famous laser light show," Lana says, "narrated by Omar Sharif. We thought it would be funny to see it."

"Omar Sharif! As a young woman, I was in love with him."

Lana gives the barest of smiles, leans back in her chair.

"We arrived by taxi on a moonless night, everything so dark. Where are the pyramids? I kept asking. And then, suddenly, as my eyes adjusted, there they were, looming directly overhead."

"You are a professor, then?"

Lana doesn't answer. Instead, she points at the wall above Milagros. "University of Miami mathematics?"

"What?" Milagros seems confused.

"The diploma there," Lana says.

"Oh, that! You do notice everything. Well, that there is a forgery."

"A what?"

When Milagros stops laughing, she says, "My daughter photoshopped it for me a few years ago."

"You didn't go to university?"

"Oh, university, yes, but in Havana, also mathematics. I was not allowed to go to Miami, you see," she continues. "My family was progressive, after a fashion. But not sufficiently evolved to protect me from the old ideas. So it was that my younger brothers, dolts and petty crooks both of them, were allowed—encouraged, actually—to move abroad to study at the University of Miami. The eldest was the stupidest, dropping out after only a year and returning to Havana to join the barbudos—that's how I knew they were going to end up being no good—the barbudos, I mean—though I supported them at the time. That's before I understood that Cubans love their dictators, all of them, love them so much that they produce them like plastic dolls, in a series. We breed them in our families, little know-it-alls, manda-mas. And the best of them graduate to politics and the very best go and make revolutions. My brothers were manda-mas pretenders, like the rest of them. Overnight, they went from supporting Batista to supporting Fidel. But neither brother was sufficiently intelligent to make the leap to full-fledged national-level tyrant like their heroes. The youngest one, Francisco, wouldn't have even made it out of college without me. Every month, an airmail package arrived at our house in Havana, a nice thick packet full of his theorems and equations. I did all his work for him, every last calculation!"

She twists her body to gaze up at the diploma. "So I guess that's not entirely a forgery. I did receive an education from the University of Miami." She turns back to Lana. "It's just that the real diploma will always celebrate my brother's name!"

———

It was a client on the Malecón who suggested it, a businessman who claimed he was visiting from Venezuela, but from his accent I knew he was Cuban, and from his shoes I knew he was from Miami. I had heard about similar arrangements of Cubans finding secret passage to Miami—no one called it *smuggling*—but I never considered it for myself. I didn't enjoy the money or connections that could make it possible. Also, I was scared. I've always been a coward, that's true. There was no way I could do it.

But that evening, over dinner, I mentioned it to Mamá. I don't know what made me tell her. Was I trying to gain her approval? Had I, in a secret part of myself, already made the decision?

"I met someone at work today who said he could get me to Miami," I said. We were sharing the diplotienda picadillo.

Mama kept eating as if she hadn't heard.

"They use a fishing yacht out of Key West, all very discreet. No more than eight passengers. Overnight trip out of Cojímar. He gave me references and everything."

Mama put another forkful in her mouth. She still hadn't looked up from her plate.

"But it's so much money that it's not even tempting," I said.

She nodded, the first indication that she'd been listening. "Most of the money probably goes to bribing some desgraciado at this end," she said.

I expected her to shake her head and shout, Absolutely Not! I, her only son. She, a widow. Her response surprised me.

"How much?" she asked.

I named the price. "I'd have to work ten years to save that much."

Mama continued eating. After a moment, without looking up at me, she said, "I'll call Mario, maybe he can help."

"Mario? That stingy old bastard wouldn't even buy us postage," I said, astonished that we were making plans in this way already.

My mother put down her fork and wiped her mouth.

"You're wrong there," she said. She stared at me for a moment as if considering if she should say what she was about to say. "After your father died, he was the only one who sent money. And he kept sending money every month for a year after. How do you think we survived the special period?"

I sat with my mouth open.

"Who do you think paid for the roofing tiles?" she said. "He didn't want me to tell anyone, not even you."

"Why?"

"He was afraid his wife would find out. I don't know. That others would ask for money. There's a lot you don't understand," she said. "Don't be presumptuous."

A month later, my uncle wired the money to a bank in the Caymans, with me promising to pay him back within the year.

At Los Ambos Mundos, a man bought me a mojito and gave me instructions. The U.S. had an amazing policy, something out of Carpentier, a policy I didn't completely understand at first: If your feet were dry, you got to stay, but if they were wet, you had to go back to Cuba. The goal was to make it to land as soon as possible and then vanish. The yacht would drop us half a mile out, before daybreak. We were to swim toward the city lights.

"Start training now," the man told me. "Get yourself nice and strong, papi."

"Mamá," I said before I left, "I'm coming back from La Yuma, with a suitcase full of steaks and a tub of butter for a feast."

⸺

The windows are open. Lana mixes colors for the mouth, a dab of yellow, orange, white, a smear of red. She holds the knife up to the canvas. Starts again. More red, the tiniest hint of blue. With a small brush, she outlines the shape of the lips, fills them in. She darkens the mix and with a few careful strokes caresses the edges to create the illusion of fullness. She leans back. With another brush, she adjusts the shape. She lifts the corners into the slightest of smiles. She wipes the brushes and leans back to look at the face that is emerging: lips lightly parted as if he might speak.

"There's a bird here," she says. "It whistles in the morning, like you used to. I haven't seen it, but I hear it now and again. It took me a while to recognize the tune, but it's a perfect mimic of the car alarms that used to go off at all hours when I was a kid."

Lana hums it. After a moment, the mockingbird responds, *"Beep beep beep."*

⸺

My uncle found me the rental, and I moved into the Helena on a Saturday morning. The furniture was already here. All I brought was my little Cuban cardboard suitcase. Those first days, I left the building only to buy food at a bodega down the block. Most nights I spent in the company of my yellow suitcase: sifting through the photographs that Yoni had gathered for me before I left. Writing letters.

I got a job washing dishes at the News Café. I'd get home in the early morning, hands red and raw, and I'd sit with the yellow suitcase until I grew sleepy. One night, feeling lonelier and more restless than usual, instead of going straight home I took a walk up Ocean Drive, following the music. At the Palace, the crowd spilled into the street. David Guetta's "Sexy Bitch" on repeat. The night refracted in the pink fluorescent glow of the marquee. Beneath it, angels danced, angels in thigh-high glitter boots and disco balls for hats. Angels with wings that reached the ceiling. The music was inside me now, all the inner workings of my body—heart, lungs, blood—pulsing to its beat. And the angels spread their gossamer wings and danced and danced. It was the first time I felt genuine happiness since arriving, and I wonder now, if I had surrendered fully to it, if I had merged with the movement of those ethereal bodies, might I have saved myself? *Don't be so afraid of pleasure, querido.*

Instead I walked home alone, climbed the stairs, and opened my yellow suitcase, where I sat again with the old photographs and the letters, buried in the past, dead, already, to the unfolding now.

⸻

She wakes very late to the sound of pounding at her door. She puts a hand to her head. Her face is swollen.

She ignores it as long as she can, but finally rises and looks through the peephole. She opens the door a crack. It's Bata de Casa.

"I hope you'll forgive me."

"Hello," Lana says. "Fefa—is that right?"

Bata de Casa looks surprised for a moment and then she nods. "Fefa, sí, a la orden."

"Please stop pounding. I'm busy right now."

"No, no, I just wanted to apologize for my . . . for the welcome I gave you."

"Okay, apology accepted," Lana says. She's about to close the door, but Fefa holds out her hand.

"See, he was young, and he didn't live through what we did."

"It's okay, really . . ." Lana begins. But Fefa doesn't move.

"Imagine someone awful comes to power in this country," Fefa says, "begins to change everything, begins to divide the country, to shut down the press, to co-opt the courts. Begins to wreck your institutions one by one. Installs his family members into positions of power. All for the glory and profit of himself. Those who disagree can leave. Or go to jail. Or be at the wrong end of the police clubs. How would you like that?"

Lana leans her head against the doorframe.

"And then, when your parents finally decide the country has abandoned them and they apply for exit, the neighbors gather outside your house—your house! The house that your father built, your own father who didn't make his money from bolita or prostitution or gun-running, who was a hard-working Gallego whose stores sold good products and who was so frugal he was able to put together another store and then another, and build a decent house for his family. For your mother and your brother and your sixteen-year-old self, who now stands inside the house your father built with honest sweat while a mob gathers outside shouting, *Worms, Worms, Worms!* What would that be like for you? Would you be able to forgive? Would you be able to forget the sight of your father? The way his hands shook when he lowered the blinds? Tell me!"

"Ma'am . . ."

"It has not left me," Fefa says in a whisper. "Half a century, and the bitterness has not left me. Not everyone understands . . . My father lost his first country to poverty and his second to thieves. My parents never regained their status here. Some exiles, you look at them, it's like they picked up where they left off. Houses in Coral Gables, servants, good cars. My parents were not like that. They emerged from exile . . . broken. My mother went to work at a shoe factory. Can you imagine! Gluing soles. And after that it was a plastics factory. And finally as a cashier at Sedano's . . . My father died in 2007, of colon cancer. At the end, he and Fidel were probably wearing colonoscopy bags at the same time. Fate has a sick sense of humor. And that son of a bitch is still alive, and my father is dead. Do you know . . . two days before my father died, he called for me. Not for my brother. He told me to come alone. Imagine. I did not want a bedside confession. I didn't know what to expect. He was . . . forgive me . . . one moment . . . he was . . . so small in the hospital bed. Wrists so thin. He told me to listen to him, that in the second drawer of his nightstand, in a green folder wrapped in string, was the deed to his burial plot. There in Woodlawn Cemetery on Eighth Street, where Machado and Somoza and Mas Canosa are buried. That's where we buried my father on March 13, 2007. He'd reserved the plot in 1976! He knew this was where he was going to die. Miami, Miami is where we will all die. Even Lenin. Even Lenin dies, and is resurrected in Miami!"

Lana looks at Fefa, her lips pressed together.

"I'm sorry," she says softly.

There were many days I could have died. What if it had been that other Tuesday morning instead? Another fruitless interview, this one at a bank downtown, finally a chance at a respectable job. Running late, I was already sweating beneath my expensive suit, I tried to put the figure out of my head, but it would have been enough to feed my mother for a month. *Investment.* That's a word I learned in Miami. Investment—the word reminded me of holy robes, the cloth a believer inhabits with hope of rewards in a next life. Halfway to the MacArthur, I realized I'd forgotten my wallet. I hesitated. Maybe I didn't need it. But then the idea of flashing lights in the rearview mirror. Of having to produce my ID. Of where-are-you-from-and-no-proof-of-my-name. At the next light, I made a U-turn. I double-parked outside the Helena and rushed up the stairs. Armpits soaked by the time I took the wheel again, wallet snug in my back pocket. At the

MacArthur, the traffic suddenly congealed. I inched along, the digital clock in my thirdhand Honda Civic racing cruelly, eating up the numbers. Sirens. When I finally crawled past the crash scene, I barely registered the stretchers, the two cars on their backs like beetles, a third flattened against the containment wall. I would be very late now. And this job I wouldn't get, either, but I drove anyway, in a rage, and did not even notice the bird that circled above, holding up the entire sky.

Lana baits the traps with cheddar cheese. Again nothing. One morning, she surprises a fat roach and screams. Within minutes, Yolanda is at her door, face twisted with worry.

She laughs, relieved, when Lana tells her about the roach.

"Ay, cariño, mice don't really like cheese—that's only in the cartoons," Yolanda says. "Mice are like us. For them, there is nothing more irresistible than sweets, and of the sweets, nothing more irresistible than junk food."

That afternoon, Yolanda returns with a bag of peanut butter cups. "Trust me," she says. She unwraps four cups and places one at the back end of each trap.

"I'm afraid all it will catch is more ants and roaches," Lana says. "Maybe I should just wait for the exterminator."

Yolanda shakes her head sadly. She holds up one finger and addresses the ceiling. "Did you hear that, young mice? This is your last chance to go on a nice vacation while you're still alive."

The following morning, every trap holds a sleek little white mouse.

———

"Lab mice," Yolanda says. "They must have escaped from somewhere."

From then on, they refer to them as the refugees.

First, Lana feeds the mice dried spaghetti through the air holes. Then, when she loses her fear, she opens the gate just wide enough to slip lettuce leaves underneath.

———

"The refugees look at me forlornly," she tells Yolanda. "As if judging me. I swear they give me an exasperated look before they return to reluctantly munching on the greens."

"What did you expect?" Yolanda says. "You tricked them! You promised them a lifetime of peanut butter cups and then treated them like rabbits."

"What am I going to do with them?" Lana says. "I'm not in any state to take care of them."

"I'd take them, but I travel too often," Yolanda says. "Maybe you can release them in the alley."

"They'd just come right back."

Yolanda bends eye-level with the traps and cries out. "*Look, mujer,*" she says, pointing to the droppings. "You'll have to do something soon."

"I know," Lana says.

———

After she has fallen asleep, the click of the front door. Moonlight bathes the apartment.

Lana lies very still in bed, straining to open her mouth. She is trying to scream, but only small cries emerge. Her limbs go rigid again. A shadow falls over her face, her own suffering. And I know I must take its place. A cold wind whistles through the open window, and then I feel her heat on me. She feels my enfolding arms. Whether we pass from reality to dreaming or into another realm altogether, we cannot say. But after a moment, terror gives way to ego-less peace, and we allow ourselves to sink into the embrace, moved, as we are by an overwhelming feeling of love.

SHE WAKES, GRADUALLY, TO FIND HERSELF LYING, not in her own bed with its bunched comforter and a view of the moon in the window, but on the couch, where, sometime in the night, she has stumbled, arranging the pillows to make space for the weight of her body.

The face is taking shape beneath Lana's touch. All morning the sound of her mixing paint, the scrape of brush on canvas. She steps back, regards the still-blurry features.

"I miss you, Milo," she says. Her eyes are wet as she strokes her brush over the image emerging from the background.

"I had another of my episodes last night. Asleep, but dreaming I'm awake. The sound of the front door opening, something entering. But I cannot move away. Paralyzed in bed, I could make out every detail in the room. The night glow on the white dresser front, the bunched comforter at my feet, the gently moving curtain at the window that holds the barest smile of moon. I am awake, I am sure of it, but I cannot speak or move, not dead but not fully alive."

She mixes the paints slowly, raises the brush over the canvas.

"Then, though my back was turned, I sensed movement. Someone entering the room. Some *thing*. And I knew that this presence meant me harm.

"I tried to scream, as always, I tried to scream, knowing now it was a dream, trying to wake myself up. But though I could feel the strain of my muscles, no sound emerged from my mouth. And then, as I was giving up hope, I felt your arms around me. I felt your warm arms around me again, and I woke."

———

Yolanda pushes sideways through the door, a huge cage in her hands and a bag hanging from her shoulders.

"I bought some things for the refugees," she says.

Lana watches as Yolanda clears two rows of books and removes one of the shelves.

"There," she says. "Instead of TV, you can watch the mice."

"Oh my god, this cage!" Lana says.

"Right? It was the fanciest cage they had, only the best for the refugees," Yolanda says. "Also, it was the last one left.

Doesn't it look like some deluxe apartment building in the Gables? Look: Three levels, and five exercise areas. This is major mouse luxury!"

Yolanda holds up the bag. "And here is some shredded paper for the bottom of the cage and enough kibble for a week. Until you decide what you want to do with them."

Together, they move the traps, tilting open the doors and letting the sleepy mice tumble butt-first into the cage.

"I don't know," Lana says when they're done.

But she's watching the mice, and there's a bare suggestion of a smile. Yolanda sees it, too.

———

Yolanda comes by every other day now, with the excuse of looking after the mice. She feeds them, cleans out the cage.

"I'll be gone next week," she says. "You'll have to figure this out."

"Where are you going?"

"Cuba," Yolanda says. "Didn't I tell you? I'm a goods agent."

"What is that?"

"Like a courier. Most of what I take these days is clothing. There's a store in Hialeah that you've never heard of. Everything they stock and make—everything is for consumption in Cuba. The most common orders I get now: What do you think they are?"

"Designer clothes?"

"School uniforms, mujer! The government provides just

two uniforms a year, and the kids plow through them. What child in a tropical climate can keep a shitty pair of uniforms clean for a year? The Cuban government, as usual with their head in their ass, can't increase production. But Hialeah can!"

Lana shakes her head.

"It all started as a favor. I was trained as a doctor—can you believe it? It's true. But then I moved to Miami, I couldn't practice with my degree. Spent all day studying for the test and nights washing the floors at a clinic in Little Havana. About two years ago, a friend of mine asked if I wanted to travel back to Cuba for a few days. Easy flight through the Caymans. So I said, Of course! I sent my mother money every other month. But I had not been back to visit since I left. This friend, he said he would pay for my ticket, all I had to do was deliver a suitcase to his cousin in Havana. Well, I didn't for a moment believe that it was really his cousin, but whatever. I said yes. And I didn't even ask for extra payment! Later, I learned that you could make a good living this way . . . I don't like the term *mule*; we are not animals. I'm a goods agent, like I said."

She reaches into her pocket and hands Lana a crumpled card. "Look, that's what it says on my business card. You can keep that . . . Maybe you know someone who could use my help."

"I don't know anyone in Cuba," Lana says.

"Mujer, if you live here long enough, you'll know someone in Cuba, trust me."

"It's not dangerous work?"

"Dangerous! Please. Sometimes the nosy Americans want to know why I travel to the Caymans so often. I tell them that I deliver goods to my family in the Caymans because they're trying to start a business. Business, the Americans respect that. The Cuban agents, I tell them I'm bringing medicines and clothing for my sister's children . . . Even the stupidest miliciano gets a little involuntary crinkle in his face when you say that. Not so much about lying, really. You just have to understand what kinds of stories people want to hear."

"You'd make a good mole," Lana says.

"Mole, mule, why is it always some animal?"

"You're funny," Lana says.

"First paying customer was a big shot in New York who was down for the winter. I think he was putting together a jazz club in Havana. That is just my speculation . . . the suitcase was full of tablecloths and glasses, everything carefully wrapped."

"You opened the suitcase?"

"Ay, mujer, you have little birds in your head!" Yolanda says. "Of course I opened the suitcase! I opened each package. Still do. I'm not an imbecile. I'm happy to help people out. Not everyone has the time to travel down to Havana three times a month. I understand that. I fill a need. But I'm not going to go to jail because some idiot wants to smuggle drugs or guns."

Yolanda watches the mice for a moment. "So I made a few deliveries for the guy and then he asked me to visit him in New York. He sets me up in some old hotel in Chelsea.

Supposed to be historic and charming. Late in the evening, after he'd returned to his wife, I lay in bed reading. Past midnight, I was woken by the shuffle of little feet. A mouse, a cute gray one with pink hands that gestured just like this one is doing right now."

Yolanda puts her pinkie through the mesh of the cage and wiggles it.

"That gray mouse stood there in front of me moving his little limbs back and forth," she says, "but at the time, I didn't understand what it was telling me."

"What was it telling you?"

"To pay attention, mujer!"

———

Lana finishes shaping the ear. She sits back. Puts down her brush.

"They're all a bunch of busybodies," she says. "But you would like them. There's a young woman, beautiful, who says she deals in goods. Most likely in information . . . I'm careful with her. A baker who reminds me of my grandmother. And there's one, an old woman, who reminds me of you. She's funny in a tragic way. The kind of person who would embark on a project to save the world and call it research.

"You wouldn't recognize me now, Milo. Talking to strangers and taking care of unfortunate creatures. But it's something you would have done."

———

That afternoon, Lana knocks on Milagros's door.

Candelaria lets her in and Milagros shouts from the living room, "What? The veteran bothering you again?"

Lana takes a seat across from her.

"No, no, he's been quiet," she says. "I had a few minutes, and I thought I'd stop in. So, what would you like me to read?"

Milagros is still for a moment, and then she claps her hands.

"I knew you'd come! You can start there, *Explosion in a Cathedral*. Do you know Carpentier?"

"I don't," Lana says.

"The father of the real marvelous," Milagros says. "Imaginary numbers, but in literature."

Lana takes the book propped on the side table. She turns it over a few times and then opens it. She begins to read. After she turns the third page, her cadence slows. Carpentier's prose is like someone weaving a heavy carpet. Lana grows more and more sleepy. After she's read the same passage three times, Milgaros notices and sighs heavily.

"Well, perfect," she says. "Let's leave it there. Carpentier one must take in small doses. It's a very powerful medicine."

Lana closes the book and stares at the cover: billowing smoke over a dark doorway. "It's not strange that I'm reading it to you in English?"

"Not at all," Milagros says. "I already read it in Spanish!"

"So why bother, then, with a translation?"

"Why bother with travel? Why bother to get to know

other people? Simply for another perspective. So you remember that there are many ways to say the same thing," Milagros says. "The English gives me new insights into the book. Though I have to say that I prefer the Spanish title: *The Century of Lights* is so much more evocative than *Explosion in a Cathedral*."

Lana makes a face. "I don't know," she says. "*Century of Lights* sounds like the name of a department store."

Milagros laughs. "Well, there, you see what I mean? Different ways to look at the same thing. To me, *Explosion in a Cathedral* is unnecessarily violent. Like the English themselves!"

"In that case," Lana says, "the English title is truer."

Milagros nods. "Ever since 9/11 it's been one explosion in a cathedral after another."

"Miriam told me about your attack back then."

"Attack?"

"The racists who threw a stone through your window."

Milagros brings a hand to her right eye and laughs.

"Oh, I thought you were talking about a heart attack or something, and I thought either Miriam is chocheando or I am," Milagros says. "Racists, eh, that's what Miriam told you?"

Lana nods. "It was because of your last name, no?"

"That's what Miriam assumed," Milagros says. "We see the world through our own experiences. It's a kind of shorthand."

"She made it up?"

"No, no, not at all," Milagros said. "She gave me the idea, and that's what I ended up telling the police. That some voices shouted, 'Go home, terrorist!'"

"I'm confused."

Milagros takes a deep breath. She looks at Lana for a long time.

"A decade's gone by," she says. "If you can keep a small confidence, I'll tell you."

Lana nods.

"I don't think it was a racist," Milagros says. "At least it wasn't an *unknown* racist."

"Not following."

Milagros sighs. "You see, I'm almost certain it was my brother, Frankie."

"What? Your own brother?"

"Well, I can't be one hundred percent sure, but I'm fairly confident."

"Miriam said the police never solved the case."

"Of course not. Because I never told them what I suspected."

Milagros clears her throat. "You have brothers or sisters?"

"A brother, in Michigan."

"And you get along?"

"Well enough."

"Well enough!" Milagros breathes a half laugh through her nose. "Because you didn't go through a revolution. Most families are never tested. Revolutions. That will test you. You have time for a story?"

Lana nods.

"Frankie was in with the barbudos, as I told you. Most of the world's problems are rooted in complejos, and by that

I mean, male complexes. Have you noticed that most of the stories men tell are about how smart they are and how stupid everyone else is? It must be a burden, to always appear the big guy. But it's more of a burden to the rest of us, really. How much violence springs from the wounded male ego—it's almost impossible to fathom. These wars now, it's complejos all the way down."

Lana looks down at the book, still in her hands. She sets it back on the table next to the photo of the young Milagros.

"Have you heard that saying, The revolution eats its children? Well, the revolution *devoured* Frankie. One of his best friends gave him up. And you know why? To get at his wife. It was biblical. Frankie spent ten years in prison. They had all sorts of stuff on him. That he had mimeographed anti-revolutionary propaganda, had ties to the CIA, aided the rebels during Bay of Pigs . . . Who knows? It might have even all been true. By that time, I had distanced myself from him. For his own good, really. My husband and I filed to leave the country and we didn't want to taint him. We left for Madrid on January fifth, 1965, a Monday. He'd been in jail by then for almost four years. They didn't let me see him. Or rather, they said he didn't want to see his gusana sister. Did he really say that? Again, who knows? The revolution eats the truth, too . . . Am I boring you, querida?"

"Not at all."

"I returned to Havana for the first time during the Carter reunifications at the end of the 1970s. Let me tell you, Carter did more for Cuban families than all the other aprovechados put together. The Cubans here think the Republicans are their best friends—my own daughter thinks this. Why? Because the Republicans talk. Cubans love talkers! That's why we're whores for dictators. For the Cuban, all reality is suspect, the only thing with the ring of truth is propaganda."

She stops and fixes her eyes on Lana.

"Forgive me if I insult your politics."

"No, not really," Lana says. "Though it's probably more complicated than that, don't you think? Symbols matter to people. They're a kind of poetry."

"Bah! Maybe you're right—I never understood poetry," Milagros says. "I look at the world and see numbers. Cause and effect. Things add up or they don't. Anyway, Frankie came to pick me up at the airport. I walked right past him. It wasn't until I took a hard look at the old man yelling, "Mila, Mila," that I realized who he was. He embraced me, but the days I spent in his moldy rooms were confusing. He alternated cool and warm. Maybe he thought we were being watched. He was also drinking a lot—one Frankie in the morning and a different one in the evening. I left that time with a void inside me. Then, in 2002, I get a call from him, he's been in Miami for two years, he says, staying with friends. Murky story of how he got out. I made the mistake of inviting him here for lunch. And of course, the first thing he does is ask if he can stay with me for a while . . ."

Milagros closes her eyes and lets her head fall back on the chair. She takes a deep breath. She is quiet for so long that she seems to have fallen asleep. When she begins again, her eyes are still closed.

"I was divorced by then, and took back my own name, restoring it to myself . . . My daughter was out of the house, already married. There was talk that the building would go condo, which meant I'd be able to buy my apartment. For the first time in my life, I enjoyed real freedom. Libertad, that thing our men are always talking about, while being so eager to snatch it from us."

She opens her eyes and turns to Lana, smiling.

"I'm talking a lot, telling you my whole life," Milagros says. "Do you have that effect on people?"

"What do you mean?"

"Of course she answers a question with a question. I'm going to believe the rumors."

"What rumors?"

Milagros laughs. "Never mind. I've known others like you. As quiet as a confessional."

Lana returns a tight smile.

Milagros waits for her to say something. But after a while, she picks up her story again.

"I never had the luxury of solitude," she says. "Maybe your generation takes this for granted. But you don't know what it's like to always have Mother and Father ordering you around, and then brother and then husband, everyone telling you what to do. And suddenly there it was: I only had Milagros to answer to. Milagros answers to Milagros! I guess it was like a drug. He looked awful, Frankie. Un verdadero gargajo. But, in the end, I said no, I said I couldn't take him in. And he went crazy. He started yelling, reminding me of everything our parents had done for me—as if he somehow inherited their karmic ledger! He left, slamming my front door behind him like a child. And that very night, the stone flew through the window. There was a terrible storm raging, and at first I confused the sound of shattering glass with thunder."

Milagros takes a deep breath at last. She brings her hand to her eye. "He died soon after. The police came to see me. My address was still in his wallet. A bar fight not far from here, in one of those dumps on Washington Avenue. He'd pulled out a knife and the other guy pulled out a gun and shot him in the chest."

Milagros turns away.

"It was a suicide, really, just like the boy who died here," she says. "Suicide is our one great national pastime. Our Cuban curse. A virus leading back all the way to the Yumurí, who, rather than submit to the Spanish, linked arms to leap the precipice; Eddy Chibás, Haydée Santamaría, Belkis Ayón, *there are burdens with which you cannot live or drag along.*"

Milagros is quiet for a long time. "I know we don't exist alone in the world, I know that," she says. "But I've never been able to reconcile my life—my competing impulses. The desire to be part of the world, to be of use; and the desire to draw the blinds, seal the cocoon, wait it out, alone."

She turns back to Lana.

"Do you know what I mean? To help or to run. I still

wonder. Could I have saved them? The brother I turned away and the boy I never spoke to. Was it my fault?"

Lana's face goes pale.

They sit like that in silence for a while until Milagros shouts: "Candelaria! El café!"

Lana wakes at five in the morning and listens in the dark. After a moment, she rises. The mice are furious at their wheels. It's the squeaking of the gears that has woken her. But she turns slowly, as if sensing something else.

Carefully she removes the bottom tray, as she's seen Yolanda do. She reaches in to wipe down the wheel and when one of the mice runs across her arm, she names him.

"You must be Toby," she says. "Yes, Toby is a good name for you." Lana replaces the bedding, refills the water bottle, and pours fresh kibble into their little tray. The mice watch from a corner. At last one of the mice approaches again and Lana takes him in her hand.

"Well, hello, you. I'll call you George. There's always one who's the friendliest."

Yolanda's at the door with another bag of mice kibble.

"I took a chance that they'd still be here," she says.

Lana points to the cage. The mice doze on the paper, their coats sleek with health.

"You cleaned it up!" Yolanda says. "So, are you going to keep them?"

"Maybe another week," Lana says. "This is Toby, that one there is George, this one is Karla. And the fat one there dozing, that's Control."

"You named your mice after characters in John le Carré?"

"You know John le Carré?"

Yolanda puts one hand on her hip. "Mujer, I came from Cuba, not some cave."

"Sorry," Lana says. "Of course."

"Don't look so sad," Yolanda says. And then, "So, spy novels? You like them, huh?"

Lana shrugs. "Not in general. But le Carré is entertaining."

"Right."

"Sit," Lana says. "I'll make some coffee."

From the kitchen, she calls, "Weren't you supposed to be leaving this week?"

"Had to postpone," Yolanda says.

"What?"

When Lana returns with the coffee, Yolanda says, "Couldn't go this week because the family I was delivering for decided they wanted to have a mass for the ashes first."

"Now you totally lost me."

"Human remains," Yolanda says. "After clothing, that's one of my most popular courier services. The living go north, the dead go south."

"Oh lord!"

"Yolanda shrugs. "It doesn't freak me out anymore. So many of those who left want to be buried in the place they were born. Even our great composer Lecuona is waiting patiently in a New York cemetery for this nightmare to pass so he can be reburied in Cuba. Not just Cubans, either, and not just now. *Make sure my bones are brought back in a little urn so I'll not be an exile still in death . . .* So far, I've delivered five urns of ashes myself. Not Ovid's, of course."

Yolanda drains her espresso. "What? You surprised I quote Ovid?"

"Not at all."

"We had a good education. The devil himself can set up a decent school," Yolanda says. "I don't get what's so hard to believe about that. We lived in a system that made prisoners out of poets and poets out of prisoners."

Lana nods. "*So I'll not be an exile still in death,*" she says.

Yolanda stares at her for a moment. Then she laughs. "Right, Profesora. I'm the one who makes sure the bones return. Isn't there a god for that?"

"Charon?"

"That's it," Yolanda says. "I should change my name to Sharon. Sharon Who Guides the Ashes Across the Straits."

She's quiet for a while before continuing.

"Some time back, I shepherded the ashes of a pretty well-known exile. A loudmouthed hard-liner."

Lana raises her eyebrows.

"That's right," Yolanda says. "That's what all this character's pomp and bluster came to: five pounds of sandy ash. He asked that his ashes be scattered off Varadero Beach. I guess he didn't have the composer's patience—or hope. In any case, his children wouldn't agree on it. The older ones refused, said it was a request tainted with dementia. Finally, fearing a court hearing that would expose it all, the one son who wanted to honor his father's wishes appeared to give in to the family, but not before managing to extract a few spoonful of ashes, which he paid me—quite well—to scatter in the sea."

"That's an unbelievable story."

"Right? I carried the ashes in my purse, divided into two plastic pots." Yolanda smiles. "I thought it was pretty clever. Two cosmetics travel pots that I bought at Target for six dollars. Covered them with a powder puff and no one even looked at them. I checked into the old Internacional, put the pots in my bathing suit, and waded out into the ocean . . . It was so quiet there, under the seafoam . . . You know, when I was a girl growing up in Regla, the telephone connections to Miami were terrible. That's my memory of those calls: My mother yelling into the phone, No te oigo! She and her brother shouting at one another for the five or ten minutes they were allotted, every other phrase some version of, I can't hear you! And this is what I remember after all these years, not the shouting, but the silence after. We are a people separated by water and despots and bound by silence. When my uncle died, no one thought to call us. His own sister went on believing her brother was alive for five more months until the letter finally arrived, Querida Teresita . . ."

After a moment, Yolanda continues. "I waded into the sea

that day with my little pots of ashes and then dove under, let the water cover me, everything still and quiet . . ."

From the street, the sound of glass breaking. Then the air conditioner cycles on. When it shuts off again, the sound of the mice starting at the wheels.

"Maybe that's all Lenin wanted," Lana says. "To find a place where everything would be still and quiet for a little while."

═══

The fatigue came over me like a smothering wave. Sudden, total. Soon it would be a year in Miami, and nothing to show for it. Between the thirdhand car and the interview suit, almost no money saved. A few dollars for Mamá each month and the rest for the rent-food-electricity. Thinking maybe next month I'll save enough, but each week falling further behind. So weary. Not ordinary sadness; a crystallized knowledge that this tiredness that called to me was the only truth, and that I must follow it wherever it led. For some people life is not a struggle. I used to watch them from the kitchen of the News Café: the couples holding hands, the families with the little children, the gorgeous ones who count on endless days of leisure and joy. The ease of love. I arrived in Miami with the same immigrant's hope. But when we leave home, we leave the company of others and enter the country of ourselves. And the self is a most unwelcoming country to live in for long. My failures drowned me. Failure to save money, failure to find real work, friends. Love. The johns I brought

up here—faceless souls, even lonelier than me. All the days
of struggle without end. Even as a young boy, partner to the
struggles of my poor mother. Always the promise of better
days that never arrive. Is it any wonder that exhaustion should
replace striving? Do any of the women here in the Helena
know true hunger? Not even Yolanda. Maybe Miriam, who
was the only one who had tried to reach me in my solitude.
She had knocked on my door one night, soon after I arrived. I
ignored her and she never returned. What if I had opened the
door to her? What if I had let her make me cake? Si solo . . .
Everyone needs a mother, she told Lana. My sweet mother.
Does she look for me in the yellow suitcase now? Does she
trace my face in the photographs? I thought she would be
happier without the burden of me, without her brother asking
every month, *How is Lenin with the money?* The fatigue of all
that worry. The exhausting regret. What might have been.
My limbs turned to stone. Five days in bed with this fever,
and no one to see me through it. Too tired to eat or wash, or
even to go through my collection of memories. And when I
could finally lift my head, it was only thanks to the malevo-
lent energy that draws sailors to the abyss.

━━

She finishes the background: a blue sky over sandy dunes of
contrasting light and shadow, the detail so fine that I can almost make out the single grains of sand. On the hazy horizon, the suggestion of date palms. In the handsome face, only
the eyes remain indistinct. "You called us the In-Between

People," she says. "Shape-shifters who belonged neither here nor there, phantoms in the Bardo, waiting."

She paints without wiping her tears.

"The night before you died, I woke to a low hum in the distance, a muddy dawn coming in through the blinds. Something moaning out there beyond the curve of earth. I moved against you, closer, your chest cool against my back. But then, still asleep, you wrapped a warm arm around me. What fears filled me then! The world shifts; a darkness opens. Your hand now forever and ever on the curve of my hip. Your mouth . . . my sweet Milo!"

=====

I couldn't live knowing I incinerated my single chance. That's all we get, people like me, one chance. Thrown away now, no matter where I look. This sadness that returns again and again like a monstrous wave. And Mario. What would Mario say? *I told you so, these new Cubans aren't worth a shit.* I hear him again, screaming over the terrible connection: *You cursed the boy with a stupid name.* But my mother named me for hope. Hope for different worlds.

I feel my pocket for the knife and pull it out. For such a small knife, it is impressively heavy. It feels good and solid in my hand, a companion at last.

And then time crawls backward. I am washing dishes at the restaurant, indifferent to the iridescence in the soap bubbles. Walking the South Beach streets, inside myself, not seeing the moonlight reflect on dark green leaves, not smelling the jasmine, not returning the shy smiles of others. I am arriving for the first time in the darkened apartment, filled with a sudden dread that I can't explain, alone, alone in a foreign country.

And then I am in the boat's hold, the smell of mold and vomit. The darkness, the feeling of being trapped not at sea, but in space, untethered, floating in doomed freedom. The boat's rocking echoed now in a kind of dizziness, as if my kind were cursed to forever drift, even on firm land.

I'm in the Ambos Mundos, the man with the oily mustache, stirring his mojito with his index finger, stirring slow circles in the drink, telling me how he can reduce the price of my passage to Miami for a little favor.

And then, back, back, to before I exist. In the home where my mother was born, the plain pine table, pine the material of poor men's coffins. But Mamá, even as a child, more practical than spiritual; someone who laughs at omens. Every morning in winter, she crowns the table with a bowl of oranges from the grove. Late summer with mangoes fermenting in their darkening skins. Flowers, palm cuttings, offerings.

On the last day, she sits in front of the portrait for a long time. She moves deliberately today. She tears off a new sheet of palette paper and takes her time opening the tubes of paint, smearing dabs in a circle. She sorts through her brushes, selects the finest ones.

Her hand hovers over the canvas. Tiny stroke by tiny

stroke, she refines the contour of the eyes. An arc for the lid. The dark outline of the irises and then the slow building of layers: dark green and brown, flecks of yellow. In the upper quadrant, a white square that she coaxes into a window, a reflection of this window in this room.

"You never knew how well I haunted that in-between," she whispers. "Paid to observe, listen, report."

She blackens the center of each iris. "I'm sorry I didn't protect you. I'm sorry."

The two luminous eyes stare back until Lana cries out and covers her own.

I watch Lana wash the pills down with vodka. She walks around the room, back and forth in front of the bed, and then she moves into the second bedroom. She traces the face in the portrait. Touches her fingers to its lips. The clock in the kitchen ticking down the minutes. The air conditioner has cycled off. We sit in the silence in between. *Tick, tick.* The air compressor starts again, and she returns to our room. Just after midnight, she falls into bed still in her street clothes.

The click of the front door. The sense of falling, suffocating. The awful certainty that we'll die, and that it will be forever. Dread fills the room. The walls creak. Lana is turned on her side, away from the door. I join her again, envelope her in my arms. But this time, I am too late. She lies still and cool. The fury that rises in me! So much waste, so much time and love squandered in this world that I have nearly left behind.

———

Outside, it is night, and I am arriving at the Helena for the last time, the building shimmering in the moonlight. Every light blazes in apartment 2B. I enter the building. Climb the stairs. Voices. The apartment's door flung open. Someone is having a party.

"Hey!" I shout. "Hey!" But no one turns. At the piano, Eugenio just before his final asthma attack, playing a song I am on the verge of recognizing. Emily, eyes yellowed with the fever, holding out her jeweled box. Time shuffles its cards: the avocado-green refrigerator, the wall phone with its twisted coil. On the table, a gelatin mold, glowing space-age jade next to the Glo-tone tableware. An alarm clock with its blinking red lights, Lana's mice suspended mid-leap. Beneath the open windows, Eugenio playing "Mi Amor Fue Una Flor"—I recognize it now, the memory floods me.

A gust blows the cover off the full-length mirror by the door. And from the bedroom, Lana appears. She is in her white gown, her hair piled high like a crown. Her eyes open in astonishment. I step forward and take her hand, cool in mine. With my other arm, I encircle her waist. Through the open windows, the scent of night-blooming jasmine, the sound of wind in the high palms. There is almost no time now. I move and she moves with me. I pull her close to feel her heart, faintly beating.

"Who are you?" she says.

"The one sent to say that it's too soon to die."

"Where are we?"

"Home," I say.

"I'm tired," she says.

"Dance."

Eugenio plays and we move in ever-widening circles, around the daveno, past the mirror, out to the dining room table piled with sweets—the Jell-O mold, banana pudding, and tres leches cake—and back again and again, wearing the pinewood floor.

Her eyes, dark-rimmed, stare into the distance as I lead.

"Why?" she asks.

"The breeze on your skin, can you feel it? Your lungs filling and emptying to fill again—it's a gift," I say. "Don't die."

Eugenio begins a new tune. The lights shimmer. The room fills with voices and then the sound of dancers, shuffling in the steady breeze. A hundred strangers dancing with us. The piano's notes seem to reach to the sky.

Lana begins to cry and I gently rest her forehead on my shoulder.

"Don't die," I say.

Eugenio is pounding the keyboards now, the music growing faster and faster. Lana lifts her head and looks me in the eyes.

"Who are you?" she says.

"I am the one who lost her son in the war," I say. "I am the one who rejected my brother. The migrant who survived and the one who didn't. I am the one mourning a lost love."

Eugenio trills a final flourish and stands. Little Emily climbs onto the table and opens her box, spilling embers like flying stars.

We whirl by the mirror again and Lana stops. She stands before it, her face drained of color. She touches her hand to her cheek. Parts her lips. But it is my face, not hers, reflected there, our black hair shiny. Thick brows over dark eyes that now open wide. We are beautiful.

She blinks once. Turns. "You are me," she says.

A sudden crosswind sucks the bedroom door to its frame, and the ghoul below awakens.

Knock it off, you bitch! It's fucking three in the morning!

The lights flicker and then darkness falls on apartment 2B. The music stops. Now again the sound of crying.

"¡Ahora se anunciaba un gran baile de pastores!" someone shouts in the dark.

My throat closes. The floorboards bend beneath us. There is almost no time now.

I gather the last of my strength, the last warmth of life that I've been able to sustain here next to Lana, and focus it into a pinhole of will, joined to her at last. We move through the room as if through time, the years holding us in a centrifuge

We are the scent of night-blooming jasmine, we are the light in the dark building. We are the wind that knocks the glass of vodka from the nightstand, the force that shatters glass, the maelstrom that bumps and bumps the dresser until the pounding sounds from below.

I said knock it off!

The nightstand falls, spilling underwear and bras that soak now in the vodka. The kitchen cabinets empty and the plates and glasses shatter on the wooden floor. Book after book tumbles from the shelves, and we don't stop until we hear the sirens.

=====

The apartment rests. For three days, it is bathed in silence. On the fifth day: The sound of footsteps. The key in the front door. A person enters. Then another. Another day and night. The mice in their cage spin and spin. Slowly, beneath the hands of the women, the apartment is returning to order. Sounds emerge, distant music, the rustle of palm fronds, the steady falling of rain. And then the clear winter light.

=====

Lana returns from the hospital the following week, a mild blue morning in January. The light slanting just so, flooding the wood floor the way it had that morning when she first woke in apartment 2B. She finds everything as she remembers it. An orderly calm. She doesn't need to know that Yolanda replaced the plates and cups. That Miriam spent two afternoons returning the books to their shelves, washing and drying the vodka-soaked clothes, folding them into the drawers. That Milagros paid Candelaria to drive to Publix and fill Lana's refrigerator with good things: A carton of milk sits in the door. In the drawers: fresh lettuce and broccoli. Red bell peppers. Lana reaches in to pass her fingers over their shiny skins. She holds one; it's heavy in her hands. On the bottom shelf: a golden box of turrón from Spain. Lana takes a deep breath.

In the living room, someone has been feeding the mice— they lie curled in plump and satisfied sleep. And on the dining table, fresh sfouf with its sunny welcome. Lana takes a step toward it and then stops. Her eyes fill with tears.

=====

Lana lies in bed the next morning and into the late afternoon, ignoring the knocks on the door. But close to evening, she remembers the refugees and rouses herself to feed them.

George and Karla and Toby play at their wheels. Control in the corner, watching. Lana watches them back, noticing, as if for the first time, their delicate, almost transparently pink fingers, their small but distinct lives. George is the only one who looks at her when she lays down the food, a brief glance. Is she mad to call it thanks? She makes coffee and returns to sit in front of the cage, and she sits there a long time, watching the mice as they grow more and more active, until by nightfall they are at their wheels again, spinning.

Below, in the street, the diggers have returned. The rumble of heavy machinery. And when it stops, the tinny music that drifts in with the night breeze. Tonight, for the first time, she hums along.

Every day I grow weaker, my eyesight fails, soon I will return to the beginning, to the formless and orderless Word that sets the story in motion. I will pass at last, sail through eras and sunsets to say a final goodbye to the beauty of this world: the silver light on the water, the iridescent beetle in the grass, the illusions that I abandoned too soon, too soon. I wished to study the long past, as if, in doing so, I might change it. If only, I thought. If only I had been born in a different place. If I could have done different work—bank teller, street sweeper, landscaper—if I'd never left Cuba, if I hadn't accepted Mario's money, if I had never met that client on the Malecón, if Havana had not been flooded by foreign men with appetites, if foreign men had not horded all the riches, if the world had been kind, if everyone had been satisfied with what they had, if they had been willing to share, drawn up a different future, decided ahead of time that no one would be hungry. If the world had been kind, if the hurricanes hadn't come, if yellow fever had been vanquished earlier, if men had never dreamed of glorious death, if conquerors had stayed home to knit, if we had built a house with room enough for everyone. If the world had been kind. If at the very beginning all the paths had been made clear and the first man and the first woman had been allowed to inspect the plans and say this one, this is the correct way, this is the road that will take us to that world where all our children will be happy.

If only I inherited a different story . . . But I was caught in my small human vanities. The world moves forward. The past is immutable concrete, subject only to erosion. But we can alter the future, even after death, we can map a new story. We can keep one small thing alive that becomes the whole world: the small burrowing mammal who survives the monsters and the firestorms to give rise to me and you.

MORNING. THROUGH THE SHADOWS, I WATCH Lana. She has dressed and brushed her hair. Her spine is straight. Her shoulders are pulled back as she crosses the apartment. She stops in front of the cage, calling out softly to the mice. Good morning, Karla, George, Toby, Control . . . They are winding down from their night's exploits. She opens the cage and waits for George to hop onto her hand. She strokes his white fur and brings him up to her face. The animal turns to her, whiskers lazy above its tiny mouth. Lana strokes him again and again, speaking softly. After a long moment, she lowers her hand and returns the mouse to its cage; its dumb eyes seem inscrutable, but I know.

Acknowledgments

By convention, an author's name usually appears alone on a book's cover. It's a pity, because all writers know they create within a net of relationships and assorted acts of kindness. I alone am responsible for any failings in this story, but whatever is true and worthy in it is thanks to an impossibly long list of influences: other writers, teachers, friends, family, mentors, editors, agents, students, readers. I'm especially indebted to several brilliant women in my life, including my mother Maria and my sister Rosa, who read multiple drafts with her usual care and love. This book is dedicated to my beautiful grandmothers, natural storytellers whose ambitions were thwarted by tradition and emigration. Every time I write, I give thanks for the time and privilege of being able to sit down for hours and years and simply imagine. Thank you to my father Saul who gave me literature and taught me to believe in better worlds. I've spent more than a decade writing this book and would never have finished it without the constant encouragement and willingness to read every draft that the great scholar Isabel Alvarez-Borland showed. Aquí lo tienes al fin, querida Isabel. Thank you also to Ileana Oroza, friend and mentor who early on lent me her apartment for writing when my house filled with visitors. Thank you to my dear friend Diana Abu Jaber, who writes the best books, bakes the best baklava, and is an inspiration in all things. And to my colleagues at Florida International University, especially Ana Luszczynska, who read more drafts than anyone should be forced to and who has read and taught my work for many years. Thank you, Ana. And to Heather Russell, Julio Capó Jr., Rebecca Friedman, Phillip Carter, my mentor John Stuart, my dear friends James Sutton and Asher Milbauer, and the English department faculty and students who have welcomed me so warmly. To my steadfast, tireless, straight-talking, fabulous agent Joy Harris, who kept pushing me past the point of comfort: I am so grateful. Thank you, too, for leading me to Counterpoint. I could not have dreamed up a better editor than Dan Smetanka, who took every word to heart as if he'd written it himself and made the story better and stronger in every way: his authors didn't exaggerate when they told me Dan was the best in the business. Thanks as well to Dan López and the other editors and staff at Counterpoint. Mil gracias to my Cuban-American literary gang, chief among them, Cristina García (who's been inspiring me for three decades), Achy Obejas, Ruth Behar, Aminda Marqués González, Uva de Aragón, Jorge Duany, Pablo Medina,

Richard Blanco, and, as always, my uncle Dionisio Martínez, my first and greatest influence. And to John Murillo whose work and life remain a model for me. So very grateful to the incomparable Anjanette Delgado who not only graciously invited me to contribute to her edited anthology: *Home in Florida*, but who also provided the title to this novel. Gracias as well to the scholars Iraida H. López and Eliana S. Rivero for their long support and friendship. Thank you Arnie Markowitz, legendary newsman, for reading an early draft. And to Mitchell Kaplan, whose long friendship I so treasure. I am lucky to have counted as a friend the late, great Alan Cheuse, who was the first to suggest I write a Cairo novel. This isn't quite what he envisioned, but the ghost of that story resides here. I miss you, Alan. Several books contributed to the research for this novel, chief among them: *Lost Miami Beach* by Carolyn Klepser, *Miami Beach (Images of America)* by Seth Bramson, and *Miami Beach: A Centennial History* by Howard Kleinberg and Carolyn Klepser.

And finally, my first and greatest gratitude to my two Peters who keep me laughing and happy no matter where we are in the world: my husband Peter, who backs every creative whim that strikes me and whose calm humor and support have been a refuge since the first day we met in Cairo; and to our son Petriček: the most joyful, creative, and loving spirit I've known—it's a privilege to be your mom.

Credits

Portions of this book previously appeared in different versions in the following publications:

The New England Review, "Susan, 1988," excerpt. March 2022, Vol. 43, No. 1: www.nereview.com/vol-43-no-1-2022/.

Home in Florida: Latinx Writers and the Literature of Uprootedness, "The Apartment," novel excerpt. Edited by Anjanette Delgado, November 2021, University of Florida Press.

Let's Hear Their Voices: Cuban American Writers of the Second Generation, "The Death of Lenin García," novel excerpt. Edited by Iraida H. López and Eliana S. Rivero, 2019, SUNY Press.

Bridges to Cuba blog, "Can't Hear You," edited by Richard Blanco and Ruth Behar, March 27, 2017. bridgestocuba.com/2017/03/cant-hear-you/.

One World Two. Anthology of International Literature: "Ghosts," short story. *New Internationalist*, 2016. Edited by Ovo Adagha and Chris Brazier.

"Ghosts," short story. *New Internationalist*, October 2016.

© Peter Polak

ANA MENÉNDEZ has published four books of fiction: *Adios, Happy Homeland!*; *The Last War*; *Loving Che*; and *In Cuba I Was a German Shepherd*. She has worked as a journalist in the United States and abroad, most recently as a prize-winning columnist for the *Miami Herald*. As a reporter, she wrote about Cuba, Haiti, Kashmir, Afghanistan, and India. Her work has appeared in *Vogue*, *BOMB*, *The New York Times*, and *Tin House* and has been included in several anthologies, including *The Norton Anthology of Latino Literature*. She has a BA in English from Florida International University and an MFA from New York University. From 2008 to 2009, she lived in Cairo as a Fulbright Scholar. She has also lived in India, Turkey, Slovakia, and the Netherlands, where she designed a creative writing minor at Maastricht University in 2011. She is currently an associate professor at Florida International University with joint appointments in English and the Wolfsonian Public Humanities Lab. Find out more at anamenendezonline.com.